A BAG—BURIED IN THE MIDDLE OF A FIELD? Crystal gingerly cut into the burlap. She wasn't at all sure what she had found inside, except that it was heavy metal, very old, and very broken.

"Hey, Dad, come look at this!"

CRYSTAL'S SOLID GOLD DISCOVERY

STEPHEN AND JANET BLY

Chariot Books
DAVID C. COOK PUBLISHING CO.

A Quick Fox Book

Published by Chariot books, an imprint of David C. Cook Publishing Co.

David C. Cook Publishing Co., Elgin, Illinois 60120
David C. Cook Publishing Co., Weston, Ontario

CRYSTAL'S SOLID GOLD DISCOVERY
© 1986 by Stephen and Janet Bly

Cover illustration by Paul Turnbaugh
Cover and book design by Chris Patchel

First Printing, 1986
Printed in the United States of America
90 89 88 87 86   1 2 3 4 5

Library of Congress Cataloging-in-Publication Data

Bly, Stephen A.
  Crystal's solid gold discovery.

  (A Quick fox book)
  Summary: While spending a week with her father in the Idaho mountains, fourteen-year-old Crystal helps uncover a fraudulent plot involving an abandoned gold mine.
  [1. Mystery and detective stories. 2. Idaho—Fiction] I. Bly, Janet. II. Title.
PZ7.B6275Cr 1986   [Fic]   85-27966
ISBN 0-89191-604-0

CONTENTS

For Mary
who loves horses.

—1—
GETTING HER DOLLAR'S WORTH

LISTEN, NOW, DON'T TELL STEPHANIE ABOUT SHAWN, because she'll tell Sheila Edwards right away, and I want to tell her myself. And if you see Mr. Pellner, tell him I'll be out for volleyball practice as soon as I get home." Crystal took a breath before continuing her last-minute instructions as Megan's flight to California began boarding. "And . . ."

"Whoa!" Megan said as she grabbed her carryon bag and headed to the gate. "I've got to go."

Crystal waved, and suddenly Megan was gone.

The jet taxied down the runway as fourteen-year-old Crystal and her dad left the parking lot. "Well, it's just you and me kid," Mr. Blake remarked with a sideways smile.

"You and me and Caleb," Crystal added, trying to cheer herself up. With her best friend Megan gone, there'd be just she and her dad for one more week in Idaho. And Caleb, too. She couldn't forget her new prize.

The wonder of it all hit Crystal again. She was truly the owner of a horse. Surely such a surprise had some purpose. "Only God knows what it is," Crystal mused. "I sure have no idea."

During the long drive back to Kamiah, Idaho, from the airport in Spokane, Crystal set her own agenda for the coming week. While her dad researched his book, she wanted to learn to ride Caleb well enough so that she wouldn't look like such an amateur next to Patty Devers back home. She knew Patty, who had been riding for several years, would want them to ride together as soon as she found out about Crystal's horse.

Crystal also worried about getting bucked off again. "But that wasn't Caleb's fault," she said to herself. "I was the one who ran him out in front of that stagecoach. What else could he do?"

Somewhere down the Lewiston grade, Crystal dreamed about horses and canyons and multicolored wild flowers. She sat on Caleb's gray back as he walked slowly. Then he trotted. Suddenly, the trot quickened and Crystal tried to stop him. Instead of slowing, the hefty animal broke into a gallop. Crystal held on in sheer panic. Something in the trail caused him to rear back, and Crystal tumbled. She hit her right wrist. As she grabbed it and started to cry out, she felt her dad nudging her. "Come on, Crystal. We're back at the Kozy Korner Motel."

The next morning Crystal had showered, dressed, and combed her long, blonde hair by the time her father knocked at her door. Crystal LuAnne Blake was not about to oversleep today. This was the day she picked up Caleb.

The morning seemed to drag by as they decided

8

on a horse trailer. Then they bought combs, brushes, headstall, extra ropes, saddle blankets, fly spray, sweat scraper, hoof-pick, and other assorted gear that Crystal had no idea how to use.

While she was helping the clerk load the purchases into the back of the pickup, Mr. Blake walked up to her with a big hatbox under his arm. He handed it to her as she climbed in.

"Did you get a new hat, Dad?" she inquired.

"Yep, but it's not for me," he smiled. "Take a look, cowgirl."

Crystal pulled out a brightly feathered straw hat, and slapped it on her head. "All right!" she beamed with pleasure.

The A.B. Kirkland Ranch looked much different on Monday than it had last Saturday at the rodeo. Then cars, trucks, and trailers had been scattered over the pastures. People packed the grandstand. There had been noise, applause, dust, shouts, and lots of hot chili. Now the empty wooden arena stood like an abandoned village. Several workers cleaned up the grounds as Crystal and her dad drove up to the horse corral. She jumped out of the truck and climbed up the fence to see if she could spot Caleb.

Even in the remuda of several dozen horses, the big light gray one with freckles was easy to spot. As the others milled around nibbling hay, Caleb paused, turned his flashing eyes toward Crystal a moment, and whinnied. He shook his head up and down, then returned to the hay.

"He recognized me, Dad! Caleb knows me!"

One of the ranch hands walked over to them. "You folks looking for A.B.?"

"Yes," Crystal answered, "I came to get my horse, Caleb."

"Sooo, you're the plucky lady. Well, A.B.'s over at the house. If you want, I'll go fetch him."

"We'd be much obliged," Crystal smiled.

Soon, A.B. Kirkland roared up on his three-wheeler motorcycle. "There's the daredevil stage stopper!" he shouted as he dismounted. "Hey, Rusty!" he hollered. "This here's the little lady who helped me and Tommy haul in those robbers on Saturday. Can you get a headstall for me, and fetch Caleb? Bring that flowered saddle with the conchas, too. We want to set her up real good."

"I still can't believe you're giving me this horse," Crystal said, grinning shyly.

"Missy, Caleb's a good horse. But he could be a great horse if he had someone to give him the attention he needs. See here? I got forty head, and another sixty out to pasture. I need them all during the rodeo and during roundup and for the tourists in early summer. But the rest of the year they wander around getting fat and lazy.

"Now that's all right for some horses. It's all they want out of life. However, that Caleb's a different breed. He gets bored just standing around. He needs someone to work him, to ride him, to teach him new things. And just talk to him. Know what I mean? There's no way that can happen around

10

here. So I figure you're just the one for him. He's a smart horse, and he needs working with about every day. Think you can handle that?"

"Yes, sir!" Crystal replied.

Mr. Kirkland pulled out a paper from his shirt pocket. "Now, if I can get your signature on this bill of sale . . ."

Crystal stared at him. "Sale? I thought you were giving him to me!"

Kirkland laughed. "I think this is one bargain you can afford to pay for. This bill is just to make it legal. And it'll require a whole dollar from you. Wouldn't want anyone to accuse you of horse stealing, would you? Folks around here don't take kindly to such things."

"One dollar? You're selling Caleb for one dollar?" She read over the paper, then signed it. "Now Caleb's mine!"

"Not yet, young lady. Let's see that buck." He held out his hand.

Crystal dug into her pocket and handed Kirkland four quarters. Then she ran through the gate toward Caleb. Rusty showed her how to saddle him and helped her mount the Appaloosa. She led Caleb around the barn, out of the sight of the men, then attempted a few signals.

"Whoa!" she ordered as she pulled up on the reins. Caleb stopped. She scooted up in the saddle and he moved forward. This time she just used the voice command, then let the reins hang free. Caleb stopped again.

She tugged a couple of quick jerks back on the reins. He backed up. She pulled to the left, and he began a turn. She pulled to the right to reverse him. Finally, the gray stood still, crooked his neck, and peered at Crystal.

"Oh!" she cried out. "Good boy, good boy." She patted him on the side of the neck. She tried to get used to the feel of the tough hide. She kicked him, and he sauntered towards the meadow. Finally, she turned him back to the stables where the men stood talking. As she approached she planned her strategy. "I've got to ride right up to them and dismount without any help," she determined.

Rusty reached for the reins as she got closer. She shook her head. "No, thanks, I can do it myself."

She stood up in the stirrups, held onto the saddle horn with her left hand, and swung her right leg over the cantle of the saddle and the back end of the horse. "So far, so good," she sighed with relief. All she needed to do now was hit the dirt with her right foot, and pull her left shoe out of the stirrup.

Her right foot didn't touch the ground, at least not where she planned. Instead, she swung under the horse, with her left foot still stuck in the stirrup. She fell on her backside with her left foot sticking straight up. Caleb turned to stare at the sight.

She heard Kirkland say, "Well, Rusty, that's a new one. Don't believe I've ever seen someone try to ride the belly side of a horse before."

Crystal just wished they'd all go away and leave

her alone. Her dad freed her stuck foot and lifted her to her feet. "You okay, Crys?" he said, as he brushed her off.

Crystal grimaced, then tried to smile. "You mean that's not the way you're supposed to get off a horse?"

"Well, it's a little neater than getting throwed," Rusty laughed, coming over to take charge of Caleb.

Soon Mr. Blake, Crystal, and Caleb were ready to go. Crystal grabbed the rope and led Caleb to the trailer. He followed her without hesitation. She patted him on his hard nose, then closed the tailgate.

"Well, Blake, stop by next week on your way out and tell me what you know," Kirkland said as he leaned against the pickup. "I'm as curious about this gold deal as you are, and with all that fuss last weekend, it's going to be hard to keep anything secret."

"Sure will, Kirkland," Matthew Blake held out his hand. "And thanks again, for everything."

"I half expected to see Jedediah Sorensen riding up there with you," Kirkland commented.

"I asked him to come along, but he mentioned something about going to Boise to a hospital for a checkup or something. An appointment he couldn't break."

"I suppose you're not the only one who'll be missing the Sorensens?" Kirkland winked.

Crystal blushed as a picture of the blond, handsome Shawn Sorensen flashed in her mind. "I'll be much too busy with Caleb anyway," she quickly said.

"Well, Caleb wouldn't be the first horse to come between a guy and a gal," Kirkland teased as Mr. Blake turned the key, and they were off.

2

CRYSTAL AND CALEB

CRYSTAL ROLLED DOWN THE WINDOW AND LET THE cool Bitteroot Mountain breeze blow in her face. It looked like fall in this part of the northern Rockies. The tamaracks were turning yellow. They'd soon shed their year's crop of needles. Puffs of charcoal-colored smoke drifted from the exhaust stacks of nearby farmhouses.

"Northern Idaho's almost a different culture," she commented to her dad. "Anyway, it sure feels different here."

"You know the slogan," her dad said. " 'Idaho Is What America Was.' The pace of life's slower here. Notice how no one seems in such a big hurry. There's always extra time just to talk. It's a simpler, less hectic life-style. But not easier, let me remind you. It's hard work making a living here. All the same, it gives a person more opportunity to concentrate on the important things."

"Sounds like you're sold on it," Crystal laughed. "If it's so great, how come we don't live here?"

Her dad didn't answer.

By 1:30 p.m. they pulled into the community of Elk City. They stopped for lunch at Bucky's Cafe.

Crystal checked on Caleb before joining her dad at the counter.

"Crystal, this is Mr. Switzer. He says he's got a cabin for rent on the other side of the pasture, behind the cafe. He'll let you run Caleb in the pasture. How's that?"

Crystal nodded at the man in the old, beat-up cowboy hat and whiskers. "Hey, that's great. Could I spend some time riding Caleb this afternoon?"

"Sure, once we get the cabin set up. Bucky—Mr. Switzer—says the cabin had been rented out for the whole year, but the guy suddenly took off. Left the day before yesterday." Mr. Blake poured catsup on his hamburger.

He talked some more with the cafe proprietor as Crystal ate a bacon-and-tomato sandwich with mustard and dill pickle. "Is there any gold mining in this region anymore, Bucky?"

"Oh sure, some. There's always some city prospector or some kids panning gold out of the river. And about once every three years, Sun Streak comes in and dredges out the river. A young man named Thompson's digging around in the Lucky Rock, but I doubt he makes wages. The gold played out up here over a hundred years ago."

"When did the last big mine shut down?"

Bucky Switzer stroked his whiskers. "For all purposes, before the turn of the century. But Pine Mill reopened its shafts in the thirties, when labor was cheap. They shut down again as soon as the war came along. Rumor has it that there's still some good gold down there, if a person wanted to spend the money getting it out. However, gold rumors aren't worth the price of coffee in this country. If you got California plates on your rig, somebody'll try to sell you a gold claim."

"How would I go about having a look at the Pine Mill mine?" Mr. Blake continued. "I'm a writer, and I'd like a look at a real gold mine that was in operation."

"As a matter of fact, I'll have some time in the morning. I could drive you up there. It's sorta hard giving directions. None of the roads are paved, or marked. How about first thing after breakfast?"

"I'd sure appreciate that."

They left the cafe and snaked along the dirt road around the pasture to the cabin. The logs that formed it looked new. The small front porch held a couple rough log chairs.

Inside they found a living room with a double bed and wood stove. A small bedroom with a sheet covering the doorway held a single bed. Next to it was a tiny bathroom.

"This is it?" Crystal frowned. "No rug? No linoleum? No curtains? No chairs? Not even some bedding? Er, which is my room, Dad?" she ventured.

"Ah, nothing like north Idaho rusticism," he sighed with a smile. "Why don't you have the room next to the bath? Now, do you see how nice we had it at the Kozy Korner Motel?"

They unpacked in a matter of minutes. Then Matthew Blake sat on the porch with his portable electronic printer on his lap. He typed some notes while Crystal prepared to unload Caleb.

Crystal had the sensation that she'd waited for this moment her whole life. She took a deep breath full of confidence and anticipation: She now had the sole responsibility for her own gorgeous horse.

After pulling on her oldest pair of jeans and a camp shirt, tying her hair back in a ponytail, and plunking her new straw hat on her blonde head, Crystal walked out to the porch.

She relished the expanse of the green fields, topaz sky, thick forest, and immense mountains. The gentle, pine-scented breezes completed the perfect picture. On impulse she exclaimed, "You know, Dad, I think I could survive living in a place like this. Anyway, I think I could adjust in time. I'd have to get used to missing all the beach parties and concerts and things. I mean, it's rough, dirty work up here, but somebody's got to do it." She giggled.

Mr. Blake looked at his middle child with a thoughtful expression. Then he, too, stared out at the view.

Crystal changed the subject as she looked down at her grubby tennis shoes. "Dad, can I use some of that money Grandma sent me on a pair of boots?"

"Maybe so, maybe so," Mr. Blake muttered as he drifted back to his typing.

Crystal now strode over to the trailer. She opened the door by Caleb's head. He still had some hay, so she scooped it up and held it under his

18

mouth. He ate it as she patted his head and talked to him.

"Well, fella, do you realize that you have the unique distinction of being Crystal LuAnne Blake's first horse? Big deal, huh?" She leaned close to his ear. "In case you hadn't figured it out by now, I'm not a pro yet when it comes to . . . What I mean is, I don't know a lot about horses. But then, I guess you don't know much about me, either. So why don't we agree to a deal? I'll teach you about me, and you teach me about you. And if you promise not to throw me off and step on me, I'll promise not to tie little pink ribbons in your mane or put a hump on your back and enter you in the Christmas play as a camel. What do you say?"

Caleb stared into her eyes.

"Great, it's a bargain," she continued.

Crystal rummaged around in the boxes and sacks of gear they'd purchased in town and found the headstall and a four-foot green nylon lead rope. She rubbed his nose as she slowly pulled the headstall up over his eyes and ears and buckled it on him. Then she snapped the lead rope to the silver ring on the headstall. She tossed the rope inside the trailer and walked around to the rear to let down the tailgate. She raised the steel trailer bar across Caleb's rear and slapped him a few times. "Come on, boy, time to get going."

The big gray inched his way backward down the short ramp. Crystal grabbed the lead rope and led him over toward her dad.

"Well, I got him out," she announced.

"Make sure he gets some water," he advised.

"I was thinking of letting him run in the pasture while I set up. Is that okay?" Matthew Blake nodded, and Crystal led Caleb to the pasture.

She pulled him over to an old bathtub that served as a watering trough. While he drank thirstily, she returned to the pickup and grabbed an armload of hay. She fed him the hay, tossing some on the ground. Finally she unsnapped the headstall, carefully lowering it off his nose, and nudged him on the hip. "Go on, Caleb, have some fun. You had a long ride."

The Appaloosa romped away at a gallop to the far side of the pasture. Then he ran back toward Crystal, jumping high and kicking his hind legs the whole way. Crystal could see the black spots on his rump flying high above his head.

The big gray reveled in his freedom as Crystal clapped her hands in delight. Then she remembered the other supplies in the pickup. With all the gear inside the corral, Crystal sat on the tree stump and began to read a pamphlet entitled "Now That You Own a Horse."

A half hour later she finished the last page and tossed the book in a box. "Step one," she said to herself as she held up one finger, "catch the horse."

Crystal marched toward Caleb with the lead rope in hand. He stood in the middle of the pasture eating some tall hay. As she examined the horse, she remembered a silklike pink western blouse with silver fringe that she'd seen once in a western-wear store. That pink would really look great next to Caleb, she decided. Then, she looked down at her tennis shoes. "Oh, yuck! Mud!"

It wasn't mud; it was worse. She attempted to wipe off the horse manure in the tall grasses as she called Caleb. He scampered right over to her at the sound of his name, startling her. "You mean, all I had to do was stand by the gate and call?" she said in astonishment.

She put the headstall on Caleb and led him to the box of supplies, beginning a ritual that would be repeated every day for a long time to come. She tied him loosely to the rail with a slipknot that would release if he panicked. Then she combed him as she looked at the picture in the pamphlet once more. Crystal began at the neck and worked down with the circular comb, covering every inch. Next, she combed each leg. Caleb seemed to enjoy the attention as she searched for a brush.

"All right, fella," she told him, "it's time for the pedicure." Crystal was nervous about using the hoof-pick. Caleb's strong, quick legs frightened her. She slid her hand down the front of his front left leg. Caleb responded on cue. He lifted his hoof for her. She scraped out the mud and mashed weeds from his hoof and tried not to hurt or frighten him. The back left and right front were just as easy.

By now Crystal felt she had it made. But when she got to the right rear Caleb balked. He wouldn't lift his hoof.

"Now, you big lunk," she scolded, "if you don't raise that foot, we're not going riding. Understand? Caleb! Please!"

"What's the matter, kiddo?" Mr. Blake interrupted. "Got a stubborn horse?"

Crystal hadn't noticed her dad walking up. "He doesn't want to raise his hoof." She stood up, sighed, and put her hand on her hip.

"Slap him," Mr. Blake suggested.

"What?"

"I said, give him a good, hard slap," he repeated.

She wiped some stray strands of blonde hair out of her eyes. "I couldn't do that," she said.

"You'd better get used to it. You know how tough his hide is. A sharp slap feels like a gentle prod under all that hair, hide and muscle. Slide your hand down again, then slap him."

"What if he kicks me?"

"Try it," her dad coaxed.

She did and Caleb instantly lifted his hoof. Crystal smiled at her dad. He waved and walked back to the cabin. Crystal sprayed Caleb's head, neck, and rear for flies. Next came the saddle blanket and pad. Crystal centered them, picked up the saddle, and lifted it to place it on his back. She suddenly realized it was much easier to take a saddle off than put it on.

The saddle Mr. Kirkland had given her was top quality, but not light. When she raised it in the air she couldn't see the blanket. At the base of the saddle horn Crystal found a hole where the leather split to cover both sides of the frame. As she staggered under the weight of the saddle, she peeked through the small triangular hole and gave it a heave. Caleb flinched, but the saddle landed more or less where Crystal intended. She fastened the breast strap and threaded the cinch.

She worried about the bit. She murmured, "I wish I didn't have to get my fingers so close to his mouth." But the leather straps slid up smoothly onto Caleb's nose and he opened his mouth and accepted the bit. She tucked his right ear into the strap and stood back to examine her work.

She couldn't think of anything else to do, so she draped the reins over a rail and walked over to put away the box of gear. When she returned, Caleb stood waiting. His expression reminded her of something between indifference and a smile.

She jerked hard on the cinch, notched it up two holes, and then led Caleb to the gate. Holding the reins in her left hand she climbed the second rail of the gate, stuck her left foot into the stirrup, and swung her right foot over the horse. "I did it!" she beamed. "I mean, of course you helped," she quickly added, patting Caleb's neck.

As far as Crystal was concerned, she had just completed one of the major accomplishments of her existence. It ranked right next to passing the constitution test in eighth grade and singing a duet with Shawn at the recent talent show.

They explored the large pasture along the inside of the fence. It was about twice as long as a football field and three times as wide. The west side bordered the back of Bucky's cafe and several other homes and businesses in Elk City. When they reached the south edge she could see that the landscape sloped sharply into a rocky creek bed. She could hear rapids from a stream she couldn't see. A slight trail veered down toward the water. Crystal made a note to explore it sometime.

The north end of the pasture bordered the dirt road they'd traveled to get to the cabin. To the east, the forest ran right down to the fence and, in places, lapped over with a few tall ponderosa pines. After riding all around the pasture, Crystal zigzagged across the open area, allowing Caleb to trot. She jammed her heels hard into his ribs. The quicker pace threw Crystal about six inches into the air with every step and slammed her back into the saddle.

She tried to get a smooth rhythm going so she wouldn't be beaten to death. Suddenly, Caleb's right front leg seemed to give out, and he almost stumbled. He quickly pulled himself back up with a shaken Crystal. She looked back to see what had happened. She saw some loose soil that had sunk down about a foot.

"This whole pasture's covered with hay except that one tiny square, and we had to run into it. Sorry, boy, I'll watch more carefully next time." Then she looked back again.

"Hey, that dirt looks awfully soft," she said and turned Caleb around. She wanted to dismount and

24

investigate, but she didn't know if she could get off and on Caleb in one piece. She had just talked herself into not chancing a disaster and was about to ride off, when she spotted something in the deep print Caleb left in the soft, dark soil.

"Oh, rats," she said, "now I've got to investigate."

She allowed the reins to hang to the ground, then took both feet from the stirrups. She braced her hands near the saddle horn, swung her right leg off the horse, and slid to the ground. She hit the grassy ground with a thud, staggered back a step, but kept her balance. "Not graceful, but definitely my best dismount yet," she decided.

The object she had seen looked like a bag or sack closer up. She found a stick and began digging, uncovering the top of a burlap bag. She cautiously stuck her hand in the hole and tried to grip it. It wouldn't come out, so she kept digging.

She soon had the bag out of the hole. Although it was only the size of a grocery sack, it was heavy. Crystal brushed the dirt and mud off the bag, then tried to open it. A heavy piece of wire was wrapped around the open end. She tugged and pulled, but only broke a fingernail.

Crystal led Caleb to the gate and tied him up; then she ran for the cabin. She swung open the front door, and as her eyes adjusted to the darkened room, she noticed her dad napping on the bed in the corner.

"Dad!" she said as she gently shook him. "I've

25

got something to show you. Look what I found in the pasture."

He opened one eye, and she chattered on, "I found this sack buried in the middle of the field. But, I can't open it because the top's wired shut. Can I use your hunting knife?"

"A dead skunk," Mr. Blake mumbled.

"What?"

"There's probably a dead skunk inside." Mr. Blake raised up on one elbow, and ran his hand through his hair. "You know, someone hits an animal on the highway and somebody else scrapes it off and buries it."

"But, Dad, I don't think that's it. It's not squishy at all."

"Ah, maybe just skunk bones," Mr. Blake laughed.

"Come on, Dad, be serious."

"I am serious. Something smells horrible. Get that thing out of here!"

"Dad, it's my tennies. I stepped in Caleb's mess."

"Rule number one in the pasture—watch your step." He took the bag from Crystal and held it up. "You're right. It doesn't feel like a dead skunk.

"Take it out on the porch, and I'll get my knife. Just in case, I do want to open it in the open air."

He was just about to open the sack when he noticed Caleb tied to a post.

"You through riding?"

"Yes, I think so, for today. I mean, I'm kind of sure." She tilted her head toward the horse.

"Then, you'd better rub him down and get that gear off him," he ordered.

"Yeah, sure, soon as we open this . . ."

"Rule number two," Mr. Blake interrupted, "don't let anything stop you from taking good care of your horse after a ride."

Crystal jumped up. "Don't open it until I'm back," she yelled. She swung open the gate and quickly pulled off the saddle, blanket, and bridle. She grabbed the sweat scraper and an old towel and rubbed Caleb down. When the gear was all returned to the trailer, and Caleb was galloping in the pasture, she rushed back to the cabin.

She could hear her dad singing inside, "Big city, turn me loose, and set me free."

"Dad? Can I try to open the bag?" she hollered above the chorus.

He stuck his head out the small, square, open window. "Yes, but be careful. I'm getting cleaned up for dinner. But don't blame me if you get grossed out."

Crystal gingerly cut into the burlap. She wasn't at all sure what she found inside, except that it was heavy metal, very old, and very broken.

3
THE WILDFLOWER MOUNTAIN MINING COMPANY

CRYSTAL DIDN'T LOOK UP, BUT YELLED OUT, "HEY, Dad, come look at this."

Mr. Blake appeared in the doorway. He looked at Crystal's find a brief moment, then plopped down on the step to examine the parts.

"What do you think it is, Dad? It's all broken, and look at the bottom of this clamp or plate thing. It says 'Partman Bros. 1905, Denver, Colorado.' Boy, that's really old. These must have been out in that field for a long, long time."

Mr. Blake picked up a heavy iron gadget. "It looks like a printing press to me. See, you could slip a plate in here, roll some ink on it, screw down the top, and print whatever was on the plate. Of course, you could only print one copy at a time, but I guess if you weren't in a hurry. . . ."

"You sure couldn't print a very big page," Crystal interjected. "That looks only about as large as a half sheet of notebook paper."

"Yes, that is strange." Mr. Blake sorted through the chunks. "It's a quite small, portable, type press. How far is it out to where you found the bag?"

"It's right about the middle of the pasture. Why?" Crystal recognized her dad's "contemplating" look.

He got up suddenly. "Show me the place."

When they reached the diggings, Mr. Blake squatted down to examine the ground. "What are you looking for?" Crystal asked.

"Tracks."

"Tracks? Well look, here's Caleb's prints, and here's mine where I kicked in the dirt. What kind of tracks?"

Mr. Blake walked a full circle around the two-foot-squre site. "Tracks from whoever buried that sack."

"Wow, but that would have been years ago. 1905—that's even older than Grandpa."

"Sure, the press was made in 1905, but I doubt it was buried then. Remember the last time you watched them plant orange trees at Grandpa's? What is wrapped around the dirt that holds the tree roots?"

"Burlap."

"And what did Grandpa tell you when you asked him about taking off the burlap?"

"Of course! He said they just planted it down in the hole with the tree because it rots right away. But that bag didn't look at all rotted. It looked as good as new!"

"Also, look at the hay. The stand at this part of the field is nice and even, except for this one small patch. Someone's been here recently."

"Since they planted the hay in the spring?"

Her dad held up some dried hay. "I'd say more like the last two weeks. The hay that stood here in the clearing is still a little green."

As Caleb trailed behind, Crystal and her father strolled back to the gate and headed to their cabin. "While you get cleaned up for dinner," Mr. Blake said, "I'll inspect those broken plates again."

Crystal reluctantly began the search for something to wear. She grimaced to discover it was time to find a Laundromat. She knew she'd be stuck with the job of washing clothes now that Megan was gone. She hoped she could find an empty one; she hated crowded laundromats.

She washed a small stain out of the sleeve of her powder blue blouse and let it hang to dry as she showered and blow dried her hair. The only mirror she could find was was one the size of a paperback book. Finally, she was ready. She liked the way this blouse made her eyes sparkle. "All this work, and Shawn's not around to appreciate it," she sighed and went out to her dad.

"Look, Crystal," he called. "I think I've found two different styles of printing plates to go with the press. Some of these pieces have movable type. That's what makes such a mess. But look at these others. The type seems to be fused together or something. If all these were put together, we could read what it was meant to say."

"Just like a jigsaw puzzle, huh?" she commented.

"Hey, thanks, Crystal. Why didn't I think of that?"

"Think of what?" she asked in surprise.

"We'll lay them all out flat, on a suitcase or something, and try to decipher the whole mess." He picked up the bundle.

"Couldn't we wait until after dinner?" Crystal moaned. "I'm starved!"

"Sure, no hurry. Besides, I've got to talk to Bucky about that trip to the mine. And don't forget to remind me to check about Jed Sorensen."

"Do you think he's home?"

"I don't really know how long the tests were to take. I'd just like to know if everything's okay. I'll try to call Shawn at the Winchester home."

They jumped in the pickup and drove to town. "Dad," Crystal began, "if you do get hold of Shawn, could you ask him to come here and go horseback riding while you and Mr. Switzer explore the old mine? He promised to show me some things about riding. Did you know he's on the rodeo team at his high school? Hey, and girls are on it, too. They rope goats and do barrel riding."

"Barrel riding?" Mr. Blake repeated.

"I mean, barrel racing," she quickly amended.

"I'll see what I can find out," Mr. Blake agreed. Then he added, "You've sure gotten awfully independent in the last few weeks, young lady."

Crystal grinned. "I guess it's this pure mountain air. It's getting to me."

"Plus the fact of not having a mother and big

sister to keep you in line," he said as he affection-
ately grabbed her by the back of the neck. "Are you
getting rather fond of this Sorensen boy?"

"Well, I hardly know him. But, he sure is . . ."

"Very good looking," Mr. Blake finished for her.

"For sure, and he likes horses, and he's a Chris-
tian, and he's real polite and nice, and besides . . .
I've got to have something to tell everyone back
home. Won't Patty Devers just die when she sees
Caleb and hears about Shawn? Did I tell you
Patty's getting a horse?"

"Only about a thousand times," Mr. Blake said
as he turned the rig into Bucky's Cafe. They parked
next to a red Camaro Z-28.

"If we lived in Idaho, you could buy me one of
those to drive to school," Crystal giggled.

"If I were a millionaire, I wouldn't let you drive
one," he chided. "I'm going to have to fight the
boys away from your door as it is. You don't need
any extra bait."

"Oh, sure, there hasn't exactly been a line so
far."

"That's because you're only fourteen. Just wait."
He held the door open for her.

Crystal lowered her voice as they entered the
cafe. "Do you really think so?"

"It's a guarantee," he assured her as they sat
down at a booth. "All three of you girls are as
pretty as your mother, and believe me, she had
them waiting in line."

"Then how'd you get her? I mean, what did you

32

have that the others didn't?" Crystal hoped she hadn't offended her father.

Mr. Blake laughed. "Why, it was simple. I'm handsome, rich, and have a sparkling personality."

"Really, Dad. How'd you two get together?"

"The truth was, she tried to ditch one of those many other guys once, and I was the only one around whom she trusted to drive her home. I took advantage of the situation and invited her to a football game the next week. After that, we kept on dating. That was in 1961. Along the way we married, had three beautiful daughters, and became writers. Now, take a look at the menu. I'm going to call Rev. Sorensen's house."

Crystal couldn't decide between fried chicken, steak, or fresh Idaho trout. When the waitress came she asked, "Do you cook the trout with the heads still attached?"

"Sure do, honey. Do you want the trout?"

"Ah, no. I'll have the chicken. And my dad will have steak, medium rare, baked potato with butter, and blue cheese dressing on his salad."

"You know your dad pretty well," the waitress commented as she jotted down the order.

Crystal laughed. "Yep, all my life."

Mr. Blake looked worried as he returned. "What did you find out?" Crystal asked.

"I talked to Shawn. Rev. Sorensen's still down in Boise. Looks like he might have some exploratory surgery, so he'll be there awhile. Doesn't sound good. Anyway, Shawn will stay at Winchester and look after his grandfather's place. He said he might come up in the morning, but he's waiting for a phone call on the results of all the tests."

Crystal perked up. "Did you tell him to bring his horse?"

"I mentioned riding. He said his horse is down home in Riggins, but he could borrow one from a cousin who lives around here."

"I won't know for sure if he's coming!"

Mr. Blake sighed and drank some iced tea. "That's the best I could do for you. You could always come with us to the mine."

"No, I'll go riding and hope Shawn catches up with me. I'm sorry, Dad, I know Shawn will be worried about his grandpa."

The waitress brought their dinners. "Say, this is just what I wanted. How did you know?" Mr. Blake beamed.

"It's what you always order," Crystal reminded him.

"Say, did you order some huckleberry pie?"

"Huckleberry? Is there really such a thing?"

"Ah, poor underprivileged child. You've never had the pure delight of standing in the woods, among the mosquitoes and other carnivorous pests, trying to pick a gallon of those plump little berries. If someone offers you a piece of the cobbler, be sure to eat some. But my advice is to stay out of the huckleberry patch."

Crystal ordered a piece of huckleberry pie with a scoop of vanilla ice cream. The flavor was somewhere between a blueberry and a boysenberry. She really wanted another slice, but decided that was too greedy after her big dinner.

It was almost dark when they headed to the truck. They pulled onto the highway that also served as the main street of the town. In just a few moments they were back at the cabin, fumbling for a light switch. An ancient, yellowed, sixty-watt bare bulb provided the entire light supply for the living room. "Let's work on that puzzle," Mr. Blake proposed.

"Did you mention our discovery to anyone?" Crystal inquired.

"No. I want to wait until I know for sure what we have. Just so I don't ask the wrong questions to the wrong people. I'd better work on this puzzle tonight, if I'm going to the mine in the morning. You can go to bed if you want."

"No way. I'm not sleepy at all," Crystal said as she huddled with her father around the makeshift desk top they'd made from their suitcases. They sorted the pieces, putting the newer ones in one pile and the old movable type in a paper sack. The newer type was more or less jammed together into longer sections. It looked easier to assemble, so that's where they began.

Crystal counted forty-three pieces of the new plate. "I sure hope Caleb didn't do this when he stepped in that hole."

Mr. Blake carried a couple fragments over to the light bulb. "I don't think so. These two pieces seem to be pretty well flattened out, like someone hit them with a sledgehammer on a cement drive. Even Caleb's heavy hoof could only mash them in the mud, not smash down the letters."

As her dad examined the pile for more clues, Crystal couldn't help thinking he looked like an archaeologist searching for the hidden secrets of a lost civilization. "Dad," she said finally, "this is going to be next to impossible. All the type's backwards."

"You can say that again. You know what we need? Some clay. We could jam these fragments into it and keep looking for matches. Remind me to get some tomorrow." Mr. Blake yawned. "I'd better write a short letter to your mother, then get to bed. How about you?"

"Not me. I'm going to watch TV a few hours and then run down to the all-night ice-cream shop for a banana split," Crystal joked. "On second thought, maybe I'll just check on Caleb and turn in myself. Tomorrow might be a big day for both of us."

"It's pretty dark out there. You want me to go with you?"

"Oh, no. Don't bother. I've got Caleb to keep me company."

Crystal peered into the blackness that engulfed the meadow and forest. The air stood dead still. A car on the distant highway buzzing toward town sounded as though it were in front of the cabin. An animal howled deep in the woods. The sky looked immense and deep, and Crystal could see light

36

shadows from small clouds blowing across the Idaho night. As she started for the pasture, one of the clouds drifted across the moon. The howling intensified, and the shadows seemed to stir.

Crystal spun on her heels. "Dad," she said sheepishly, "It's so nice out tonight. Maybe you'd like to sit on the porch and write your letter to Mom."

Mr. Blake grinned and grabbed a flashlight. "Well, Crystal LuAnne, I'm glad you still need me for some things. Old dads like to be useful."

Crystal grabbed her father's arm and led him toward the pasture gate. Caleb stood, staring at the oncoming light. He had a stoic face. It reminded Crystal of some Indians she had seen at a reservation gift shop. She had wondered if anything would frighten or surprise them.

She patted the big gray's nose, and Mr. Blake turned off the light. "You know, Dad, it's important to me to have this horse. It's not like having another possession, like a bike or stereo or something.

"Oh? What's it like?"

"Well, for a long time I've thought of myself as a certain kind of person. That is, this may sound funny, but I've always wanted to be smart, ready for adventure and fun, and yet able to know when to get serious. But I've been afraid to let myself be that way. Afraid that someone would laugh at me, or not approve, or something. But this week, riding Caleb and all, I feel the way I've imagined myself to be."

37

"I hope you don't plan to make a career of stopping stagecoaches," Mr. Blake laughed.

"Oh, I don't think I'd ever even have the chance to repeat something like that. I wouldn't even want to. But, more than ever before I *like* me. Does that make sense?"

"It sure does, kiddo."

"Is it all right with God if I like myself in that way? I don't want to leave him out of the picture. You know, sometimes I feel like I'm not really good unless I hate myself for being lazy and self-centered. Do you know what I mean?"

"You're making more sense than many adults I know. Listen, babe, you just keep liking yourself because God's the one who made you. But make sure you're always open to his desire for some remodeling. The pressures of our world, plus our own selfishness, can misshape us from time to time. We need to be willing to be corrected. In the meantime, enjoy all the good things God allows you to have."

They walked back to the cabin with the flashlight off. The moon emerged from its temporary cover and the light from the cabin flickered over the trail.

Crystal got ready for bed, then called out to her dad, "Good night."

"Hey, look at this. I've got a word, or title, here."

Crystal crept out in her barefeet and nightgown. "What's it say?"

Mr. Blake held four sections in the palm of his

hand. "The something or other company. Mining Company. The blank Mountain Mining Company. Grab my pen and write these letters for me: *r-e-w-o-l-f-d-l-* and an *i*, I think. Those last two letters are smashed. What's that make?"

Crystal got excited. "It could be wild flower. How about the Wildflower Mountain Mining Company! Have you ever heard of it?"

Mr. Blake put the pieces down and scratched the back of his neck. "Nope, but I hope to hear something tomorrow." He began to pull off his boots.

Crystal turned out her light and lay on her back in the bed. She shivered for a moment, then warmed up as she snuggled into her sleeping bag. The only wild flower she thought about was the one she'd put in her hair when she dreamed of riding Caleb with Shawn.

4
CRYSTAL AND SHAWN

H EY, HOW MUCH BEAUTY REST DOES ONE GIRL
need?"

Crystal struggled to open one eye, then the other. She peeked out over the pile of sheets and wadded-up sleeping bag at her dad. She sat straight up, gazed around the half-lit log bedroom, laid back down, and closed her eyes.

"I just dreamed it was the first day of school, and I couldn't find my classes," she murmured. "It was horrible." She sat up again. "What time is it?"

"It's late. I've had breakfast at Bucky's already. I put some money in your purse for you to do the same. Listen, are you awake? We need to talk, I'm anxious about leaving you all alone today."

"I won't be alone if Shawn's able to come." Crystal yawned, and stood to her feet.

"And that's supposed to keep me from worrying? I don't know, Crys, perhaps you should . . ."

"Please, Dad, I promise I'll stay riding in the meadow until Shawn arrives. And if he doesn't, I'll either be here at the cabin or down at Bucky's"

"And where will you be if Shawn comes?" Mr. Blake tilted his head.

"We'll be riding around somewhere until you get back. When will you return?"

"Around 2:00 p.m., or so. Hey, I'm counting on you to make sure I've made the right decision. Remember, act smart and . . ."

"And have fun," Crystal chimed in. "Thanks, Dad. I think you're the greatest."

"Well, you must be right. That's what your mother always says when she manipulates me like you do. Eat a good breakfast, and I'll see you after lunch."

Crystal suddenly felt all alone as she watched her dad drive off in Bucky Switzer's truck. She recalled how secure she felt with her dad last night out in the dark. She missed Megan all over again. But then, she thought about Shawn. If only he's able to come, she wished.

She hurried with her morning cleanup routine and then debated blouses. "Shall I wear the pretty one to impress Shawn? Or the practical one, since I'll be riding Caleb most of the day?"

Vanity won. She chose a ruffled yellow one. "Because it shows off my tan," she concluded as she tried to get a decent view in the tiny, cracked mirror.

Caleb seemed to be expecting her as he waited by the gate. Crystal grabbed the gear box and duplicated the previous day's process. Finally, she scooped up some extra oats for him.

She got one foot in the stirrup. Caleb scooted away from her, and she hopped after him. "Hey, now, just because I spoiled you with the oats, don't go and do something crazy," she reprimanded. Caleb kept shying away. "Caleb, please!" she pleaded.

He ignored her pleas. Finally he stopped against a fence post, and Crystal swung herself into the saddle. But she couldn't put her right foot down because Caleb leaned against the fence. She shoved against the fence and pulled the reins. He stepped away "Boy, you're feeling your . . ."

Crystal caught herself in midsentence. She remembered what she'd read: "Watch out for a horse being overactive after he's eaten some oats!"

The word no more escaped her lips than Caleb galloped down the little lane leading to the highway. Crystal clung to him. "It's just like the suicide race," she moaned.

As they closed in on the highway, Caleb stretched his legs and picked up speed. Crystal shouted for him to stop. She wondered what would become of them when he hit the road. He could slide on the asphalt at this clip, and that spelled trouble for both of them. If he chose to turn quickly, she'd be the one to sail out onto the highway.

She just had to get him to slow down, or stop. She held the reins with both hands, gripped them up close to his head, and yanked back, yelling, "Whoa!" Just as they reached the road's shoulder, Caleb halted.

Crystal didn't.

Still clutching the reins, she slid up over the top of his head, and with her feet still wrapped around

42

his neck withers, slid around his head hanging upside down.

A car pulled up alongside her. Someone rolled a window down and called out, "Still having trouble with the dismount?"

Even upside down Crystal knew it was Shawn. Her blouse was half untucked, she'd lost one shoe, and part of her freshly washed blonde hair dragged in the dirt.

"Hey, look, I do a special trick for you and all I get is complaints." She tried to smile at him, but knew any attempt would just look ridiculous. "Get out of there, you creep, and help me down."

Shawn didn't move. "Turn your feet loose," he advised.

"What?"

"Just let go with your feet. You'll come right down."

Crystal released her feet and swung to the ground. She tried to straighten herself up. Shawn shook his head.

"Oats," she said matter-of-factly.

"You or him?" Shawn laughed.

Crystal picked up a handful of stones and faked a throw. "Come on, let's get something to eat," she motioned toward Bucky's.

Shawn looked down at his watch. "Supper or dinner? It's almost 9:30. What are you doing, living on California time?

"Listen, Crystal, I've eaten breakfast. I'll go get my cousin's horse saddled up and meet you back

43

here. I should be back by the time you're finished."

After breakfast she stepped out to the sidewalk. Shawn was nowhere around, so she decided to do some shopping at the variety store.

She saw her favorite brand of shampoo and spotted some clay on the shelves. She remembered what her dad had suggested and bought the clay along with the shampoo. When Crystal stepped out to check on Caleb, Shawn was beside him, riding a tall, handsome palomino.

"Hey, that's some horse," she complimented. "What's his name?"

"I'd like you to meet Grady."

"Grady? What kind of name is that for a horse?"

"Hey, I didn't name him. What's wrong with Grady?" Shawn reached down and stroked his neck.

"Oh, nothing. But a horse as nice looking as that should have a fancy name like Majestic Prince or Golden Boy or, or Benchley."

"Benchley?" Shawn exploded. "Well, this one is definitely a Grady. What do you have in the sack, may I ask?"

"Oh, just some clay," she informed him.

"Clay? You like to play with clay?" he needled.

"Sure, I make little dolls out of it and stick pins in them." She raised her eyebrows and walked over to Caleb with her nose slightly tilted. "It's for my dad, smarty."

As they rode back to the cabin, Crystal related the story of her find. "I don't know about the

44

plates, but the press was made in Denver in 1905."

As they passed the cabin and headed for the pasture, Shawn and Grady shot off straight for the gate. The palomino cleared the five-foot gate as he galloped off into the pasture. "No, way, Caleb, don't even think of it," Crystal admonished.

She dismounted with no problem. "Always when no one's looking," she sighed. She opened the gate and walked Caleb through. For the next half hour Crystal and Shawn raced their mounts around the edge of the pasture. At first, Crystal held on with controlled panic. Soon she accustomed herself to the pace and relaxed. Crystal could see that Shawn was a great rider on a good horse, and she was a beginning rider on a great horse. She was afraid to allow Caleb to fly.

Finally they slowed down and walked the horses to the pasture's center where Crystal had found the burlap bag.

"You know, there's a museum down in Cottonwood that might be interested in your discovery," Shawn commented. "You could even have your name on a plaque. However, I'll have to admit that 1905 isn't exactly ancient history."

"Do you think they'd really put my name on a plaque?"

"Oh, come on. Surely you'd rather go for the heavenly rewards instead," Shawn kidded.

"You mean you'd turn down a chance to have your name in gold or brass or whatever?" Crystal asked.

"As a matter of fact, I am wearing one of my own earthly rewards. Did you see this belt buckle Mr. Kirkland gave me? I just got it yesterday. I waited for them to engrave my name on it."

The huge buckle flashed in her face. "Hey, that is neat-o. It's got jewels and etchings and everything."

"It's certainly the fanciest one I own, and I have seven or eight others. Hey, look at the sky."

They hadn't paid attention to the dark clouds stacking up against the eastern mountains. "Do you think it's going to . . .?" Before Crystal got the words out, big drops of rain hit her face. The next instant the air was drenched in a sudden downpour.

"I do believe it's going to rain," Shawn whooped as he and Grady took leaping strides to the gate.

Crystal followed as fast as she dared. They yanked the tack off their horses. Crystal splashed through the mud to tug her saddle blankets, bridle, and the rest into the front compartment of the horse trailer. Shawn piled his gear on the covered front porch of the cabin, where Crystal joined him.

"I've got to go in and dry my hair and change. I'll be right back out," she announced.

Shawn sat down in a chair and pulled out his pocketknife. "Sure, go ahead, I'll just whittle out here in the rain."

"Hey, sorry, it's just that . . ."

"Don't worry, I understand. You don't think Idaho boys are that dumb, do you? Besides, this

46

storm will pass in just a few minutes. And I'll dry out quickly."

Crystal stopped at the door and asked one more question. "Do you think we should scrape the sweat off the horses?"

"Yep, soon as God quits hosing them off," Shawn replied.

Crystal rushed into the cabin and got the hair dryer going. "Come on, hurry it up," she coaxed the machine. "I don't want to keep him waiting too long."

She changed into her old, dry jeans and a grubby T-shirt. "Rats, I made the wrong choice this morning," she groaned, as she hung the wet yellow blouse to dry. "Oh, well, he might as well see me at my worst, too."

When she returned to the porch, the rain had slowed to a light sprinkle. She watched Shawn slice up a short stick.

"What are you carving?" she asked.

"I'm not carving. This is what you call whittling. When you whittle, you don't try to make anything. Actually, I'm returning this stick to whence it came, the ground."

Crystal sat down in the chair next to Shawn. "What shall we do while we're waiting for the rain to stop?"

"We could play with your clay," Shawn teased.

"Hey! That's a great idea!" Crystal jumped up and ran inside. She carried out the small press and broken pieces. "Help me match these up, and then we'll mash them upside down in the clay—like a holder. When we're all through, we can press them lightly into another chunk of clay and read what the message is."

"Sounds like a fascinating way to spend the time," Shawn agreed. She couldn't decide if he was serious or not.

The next thirty minutes passed in a hurry as they played with the puzzle. Shawn picked up a piece for the third time. "This has to be the one." He fit several small bits of type together and inserted them in the clay.

Crystal found the adjoining piece in her pile. Quickly Shawn had another line completed. "Now we're really going," Crystal said with growing excitement. Soon they had seven lines almost finished.

"We do have something missing up here on the second line," Shawn pointed out.

"Let's print it on the blue clay now." Crystal pounded the rectangular hunk of clay flat. They gently pressed in the type. She held the finished product up and the two squinted to interpret it.

Shawn read aloud, " 'The Wildflower Mountain Mining Company, One one-thousandth (1/1000) share of the mineral rights to the SW quarter of the SW quarter of Section 36 Township 14 Range 4, Mount Borah Base Meridan, being hereby granted to somebody or other, on this 26th day of September, 1908.' "

"I still don't understand it," Crystal admitted.

"It's like a deed, at least for the mineral rights. You know, like gold, silver, or whatever."

"But the name's missing. It wasn't blank, was it?"

Shawn looked closer. "There could have been something there, and the name was removed somehow."

"Maybe the other plate will solve the mystery."

"The other plate?"

"Yes, there's another one in the cabin more broken up than this one. Dad says it's even older. You want to try to put it together?"

Shawn stood up and stretched his arms. "Nah, let's go ride. It's not going to rain anymore."

They saddled up Caleb and Grady and traveled along the outside of the fence this time. As they sauntered slowly through the woods, Shawn spoke without looking back at Crystal. "You know, Crystal, you're really different."

Crystal's heart pounded. "What do you mean, different?"

"Well, I've known you for less than a week, and already you've been chased by the cavalry, stopped a stagecoach, been given a horse, and discovered a buried treasure. Are things like this always happening to you? I've lived here in Idaho all my life, and it's been pretty tranquil, I'd say." He stopped his horse now and turned towards her.

Crystal giggled. "Sure. Why, just last month I jetted to the Orient, wrote a symphony, starred in two television shows, had dinner with the president, and spied for the CIA." She rode up beside Shawn and Grady. "Honest, before last week the most exciting thing that ever happened to me was getting my toothbrush caught in my braces, and once I was rushed to the hospital emergency room on Thanksgiving—appendicitis."

Shawn smiled warmly and Crystal ventured to ask, "What's it like going to high school in Idaho?"

Shawn pushed his horse forward and swerved around a downed red fir tree. "Just like anywhere else, I suppose. Just smaller. There are eighty-four kids in my school; only nineteen in my class. Out of that nineteen, sixteen of them started school with me in kindergarten. We've been together all the way through. It does make for a close-knit unit, though."

"That doesn't make many guys and girls to choose from," Crystal hinted. She thought about the four thousand students at Citrus Valley High.

"True, but not only that, it's sort of like dating your sister. That is," he quickly explained, "that's what I've been told. We've known each other so long. Funny, I've never talked like this with any of them, although they're good friends. I guess because they've all been there, so they know everything."

"Sounds nice to me," Crystal observed. "I had to choose between nineteen advanced freshman English classes. Nineteen! I doubt if I'll know a single person in the whole class."

"That doesn't sound appealing to me. What I like

50

about a small school is the sense of community, and caring. It's like one big extended family. I guess I live in a sheltered world, compared to yours."

"What's so wrong about sheltered? That could mean secure, safe, cozy. But, is it hard for new kids to fit in? I mean, don't you all have your own little clique?"

"Well, why don't you move on up to Riggins and find out? I guarantee you'll know the whole school before the first week's out." He chuckled. "Give yourself two weeks and you could know every kid in northern Idaho."

"I could never get my family to move. My dad's lived right in that same house for eighteen years. Then there's my sister Karla . . ."

Shawn stopped suddenly. "Look! Bear sign!" He pointed to clawed tracks in the muddy trail crossing. "And they look fresh. Looks like he's long gone to the creek."

"Hey, I've seen that creek before. Yesterday when I rode around the pasture fence I could see a trail alongside it. Want to follow it?"

"Why don't you start down the trail? I'll ride back to my cousin's so I can see if they've heard from Grandpa. While I'm there I'll grab a couple sandwiches. We'll have a picnic at the creek bottom, down next to the river."

"But what about that bear?" Crystal exclaimed. "I can't go out there alone! I think I'll just go back to the cabin."

"That's not the same girl talking that I knew last weekend." Shawn paused and added. "Well, I'm going. What have you decided?"

"See you down at the creek," she hollered back as she nudged Caleb on.

She talked as loud as she could to the horse as she rode. "Caleb, I hope you know how to cross streams without slipping on the rocks. I've never done it myself, and I'm not sure exactly what to do. Maybe I should walk you across. No, then I'd get wet. Of course, if you fall down, I'll get wet anyway."

She continued to jabber as he trotted down the trail and across a narrow strip of sand. When they reached the creek, she let out a big yell and hung on to Caleb's neck. He forded the stream smoothly without a single stumble or slip, hurried up the slight embankment, and continued down the trail.

Crystal felt foolish as she patted him and said, "So that's how you do it. I see you've been through this before."

They came to a small inlet along the stream, shaded by overhanging trees. "This looks like a good place for a picnic. Maybe we should wait right here." She started to dismount when she remembered Shawn had mentioned a place where the creek joined a larger river. She stayed on, and they kept going.

Suddenly the creek descended sharply. She maneuvered Caleb slowly downhill, concerned about his balance the whole way. She watched his head, and at a point where the trail seemed the steepest he closed his eyes.

Crystal imagined he was frightened and didn't want to look. However, she was startled to realize that he was just dozing off as they walked along.

All of a sudden, Caleb jerked his head straight back and snorted. Crystal jumped in her saddle. She looked around for what might have startled Caleb. She couldn't see anything, but Caleb wouldn't go a step further.

Crystal got down and looked in the grass and along the trail. Caleb followed with much caution. They bended some rocks and both heard the noise at the same time. Caleb tried to lunge out of her grip. Only the knot where the two reins tied together kept her holding on. Her mind raced to figure how she could remount and exit in a hurry. A large black bear lumbered toward them.

With adrenalin flowing, she cleared Caleb's back in two mighty jumps. He twisted and turned, then reared.

"Hey, did you bring my mail?" A voice rang out.

Crystal tried to calm Caleb. When he settled down she turned in the saddle and stared. The bear was nowhere in sight.

"I said, did you bring my mail?"

5

THE BACKCOUNTRY

CRYSTAL GAPED AT AN OLDER MAN WITH A SHORT, but very full, white beard. He picked up a long stick and shaded his eyes. "Who are you?" he rasped.

"Mister, there's a wild bear back there," Crystal warned.

"A wild bear, you say? That sounds like trouble. I'd better get Sunshine." The old man climbed some rocks in the direction she'd last seen the bear. He returned a moment later leading a black bear.

"Say, this isn't the bear you saw, is it?"

Crystal shuddered and Caleb backed up. "Yes, I think so. Aren't you afraid of him?"

"Afraid of Sunshine? She's a cream puff. Comes to visit me every summer."

"Do you live around here?" Crystal inquired.

"Just in the summers. I've got my forty acres and cabin. When the snow gets too bad, I go home, where I've got a nice ocean-view condo in West Palm Beach, Florida."

Crystal relaxed with a smile. "I'm Crystal Blake. My dad and I are visiting Elk City for a few days. I'm out for a ride on the trail." She patted Caleb.

"Glad to make your acquaintance, Crystal Blake." He held out his rough, strong hand. "I'm Howard Stanton. Most folks just call me Doc." He turned to the bear. "Go on, shoo, get." He slapped her on the rear, and she waddled across the creek and into the woods.

"Are you a real doctor? I mean, a medical doctor?" Crystal wanted to know.

"Nope. I do have a doctorate, though, in geology. Before I retired I was head of a university geology department."

"You're a geologist?" Crystal said in some surprise.

"Not anymore. I'm just an old man who likes the woods come spring. Say, I'm sorry to have startled you. A fella's been coming down the trail here every Monday, and I'd talked him into bringing my mail. That way I don't have to go to town so often. But when he didn't show up this week, I thought maybe he'd sent you as a substitute. I sure hate to miss my mail." The old man reached back over his shoulder and scratched his back.

"You expecting something important?"

"Sure am. Gotta keep up with the *Wall Street Journal*, see how the market's going. Say, you don't know a tall, thin fellow by the name of Davenport, do you? He's renting that cabin at the edge of the woods behind Bucky's place."

"I don't think he is anymore. That's where my dad and I are staying. I think Mr. Switzer said he took off real sudden."

"I guess I'd better get to town in a day or so. Sorry to keep you from your trip. You go on, and if you run into Sunshine again, just give her a swat and send her home." He prepared to hike back into the woods.

A thought stirred within Crystal. "Hey, wait a minute, Doc," she called out. The man kept going. Crystal rode Caleb up next to him, and he turned around. "Mr. Stanton, have you ever heard of the Wildflower Mountain Mining Company?"

He stared at her with curious eyes. "I haven't heard that name in years. Now, there's a case that would take hours to tell of. This many years later, it sounds even funny, but at the time. . . . Well, as I said, it's a long story."

"I've got the time. I mean, if you do. My friend Shawn will be coming to meet me, so I have to wait anyway. I'd really like to hear about it."

"Well, give your horse a break, and sit down on this rock. I'll try to make it brief."

Crystal jumped down with only a slight stumble, loosed Caleb's cinch, and let him rest in the shade of the trees. She made herself as comfortable as possible while the old man did the same. As she listened, she picked up a few pebbles and skipped them in the shallow water.

"It seems like around the turn of the century, maybe late in '05 or early '06, a fella by the name of Clayton came in here and began to buy up mineral rights. By then the gold had long played out, and mineral rights were dirt cheap. Before anyone real-

56

ized, he owned about all the rights around except one or two shafts.

"Some folks got worried that maybe he knew something they didn't. Soon, it came out that he was a scientist from San Francisco and had developed a special acid which he called Chematron. He claimed it would dissolve quartz deposits that would make it possible to separate out gold. There was still some gold down in those shafts, still is today, but the cost of digging it out and stamping it down exceeded any benefits.

"However, if a miracle solution like this had been discovered, it could easily separate the rock from the gold. Then the story'd be different. So Professor Clayton, as he called himself, went back to San Francisco with samples of his work to show to potential financial backers.

"Folks, of course, were highly skeptical. After all, every gold scam known to man was tried there at one time or another. But Clayton was convincing. A geologist from the university took out a sample of gold laden quartz and used Professor Clayton's Chematron on it. It worked so well that the man wrote a highly supportive article for the newspaper and invested some money himself.

"Soon every banker and society lady in town was lining up to invest. They scheduled a get-together at the Grand Union Hotel for one final demonstration of Chematron. Well, the meeting didn't come off. Three days before the meeting the big San Francisco earthquake hit. It leveled the Grand

Union and the samples of Chematron and quartz gold were lost.

"Many days later they talked of getting together again. However, by this time half the folks had better things to do with their money and time, since the entire city needed rebuilding. Besides, Clayton needed time to make more Chematron. But the university fella said they should go ahead anyway. Said he had saved a little Chematron from the earlier experiment and would have a friend in Placerville send over quartz samples.

"Well, Clayton argued that the earthquake had made all Chematron unstable, that it wouldn't perform normally. He insisted on waiting until he could produce a new batch. However. the few investors still interested asked the geologist to go ahead. Clayton boycotted the meeting, and the experiment failed. The geologist's Chematron was useless on the hard rock."

The old man stood up, leaned against his stick, and continued. "That's when some chemists at the university analyzed the Chematron. They found it to be nothing more than hydrochloric acid mixed with some green dye. Then it leaked out that an assistant in the lab at the university had been bribed to switch quartz samples. They surmised that the earlier tested rock was really something fake that melted in hydrochloric acid.

"Now, that's the last time anyone ever heard from this fellow, Clayton. He seemed to disappear off the face of the earth. So did his mining company—the Wildflower Mountain Mining Company. He still owned all those mineral rights, but no one knew of any relatives, and he left no forwarding address. Actually, no one worried about it too much since the old shafts were worthless anyway. Except in the early thirties, when labor was cheap, a couple outfits wanted to do some exploring. As the matter stood, they called it an abandoned claim, and it was never tested in court.

"They had to leave off the exploration when the miners got called to war. As far as I know, it's still a debate who holds the mineral rights, at least until those one thousand company stock certificates reappear. If they haven't been burned in the trash by now, they're probably lining someone's dresser drawer or birdcage."

Crystal stood up to stretch. "You mean if someone had those certificates, they could claim the mineral rights on a lot of land?"

"They could sure try. But who knows? Even with $300-an-ounce gold prices, it doesn't pay to dig out what little gold's left." Doc Stanton laughed. "Of course, I guess a person could invent some more Chematron. Until that time, the gold's going to stay right down there in the ground.

"By the way, how did a stranger like you hear about the Wildflower Company? You don't happen to have one of those certificates, do you?"

"No, not exactly. But my dad and I just might have found one of the old printing plates used to print the certificates. So that's why I was asking."

The old man gave her a searching look as she peered down the trail for Shawn. She walked over to Caleb and cinched him down. Then she mounted with relative ease. "At least someone's watching this time," she said to herself.

"Thanks for your story, Mr. Stanton," she called out.

He held his stick up in farewell.

The next few minutes Crystal sat alert as Caleb threaded his way down a couple steep inclines. She feared he'd balk; she didn't know what she'd do then. However, he never once acted apprehensive.

They reached a sandy area and a narrow gorge between two tall granite walls. They passed through the opening into a wide beach area next to a roaring, clear river. The sun stood just past straight up, and only a few white puffs remained of the recent storm. A gentle, refreshing wind blew down the river canyon.

Crystal dismounted and looked around her. Mountains ascended abruptly on both sides of the river. She could hear or see no living creature anywhere. In fact, she noticed no signs of civilization: no roads, no telephone poles, no buildings. She couldn't find a single discarded can or piece of litter. She imagined herself as one of the first explorers to reach such a place.

She pulled off Caleb's saddle and blanket. He roamed around the creek inlet. Then she tugged off her socks and tennies, rolled up her jeans, and waded into the rushing river. As the water reached her ankles she splashed back to the sand. "That's the coldest water I ever felt in my life!" she gasped.

She lay down in the warm sand for a few minutes, then propped herself up against the saddle. "This is more peaceful than quiet time at church camp," she sighed, running her fingers through the sand.

At that moment a raft appeared around the bend of the river. She sat up for a better look. It was a large, inflatable rapids runner with six or eight people on board. She stood up, intending to wave at them as they passed by. Caleb cantered up beside her.

The white water rafters headed straight for her beach. She stepped back as they jumped out and dragged the boat ashore. Most of the occupants looked to be high school age, except one who carried long oars. He looked older. "Hi!" called one of the girls, "do you live around here?"

"Of course she lives around here, dipstick," answered one of the guys. "See her horse?"

"Wow! Does she ride it bareback? I've never ridden bareback."

"You've never ridden at all."

Crystal felt uncomfortable as they bantered back and forth without her getting in a word. Finally, a muscular boy with a brightly striped tank top turned to her. "What do you say, blondie, let's you and me run off to the hills and live in a small mountain cabin the rest of our lives."

A girl said, "Don't let that creep bother you.

Damian couldn't last two days without pizza."

Damian staggered out along the beach with those words, and screamed, "A pizza, a pizza, my kingdom for a pizza!" Then he fell flat on his face.

Crystal couldn't help laughing at all his antics. Then the older boy with the oars cried out, "Grab your brown bags and eat. This is a ten-minute stop. Ten minutes. Got that? And nobody wanders off without checking with me first."

He walked over to Crystal. "Hi, I'm Chad Browne. This wild group's with Final Quest. Would you like to share a bite of lunch with us?"

Crystal brushed some hair from her face. "No thanks. A friend of mine will be joining me soon with some food. What is Final Quest, anyway?"

"It's a ten-week summer endurance program for teens. Kids from all over the states travel together through remote areas of North America. Now we're here in Idaho, our last stop before home."

"Where's home?" Crystal asked.

"For me, it's Colorado. Most of the gang's from Chicago. They're not always this rowdy and rude, but it's getting the end of the trail, so to speak. They're feeling their oats."

Crystal winced.

"Hey," he continued, "you don't happen to know a man named . . ." He reached into his pocket for a scrap of paper. "Davenport. His name's Davenport."

"No," Crystal replied, "I don't know him, but I've heard of him."

"Old Scotty up at the crossing asked me to float down a ninety-pound sack of cement for the guy. It seems he bought some bags a few weeks back, and Scotty sends one down to him every week." He scanned the surroundings. "Now, why in the world would anyone want cement around here?"

"Yeah, that does sound funny," Crystal agreed. She watched as Chad strolled back to the raft, lifted a heavy plastic-wrapped bag, and tossed it on the sand. "Listen, uh, sorry I didn't catch your name."

"I'm Crystal Blake, and I don't live around here. I'm just on vacation."

"Glad to meet you, Crystal. How about my leaving this bundle right here. If this Davenport guy shows up, he'll be sure to find it. And if he doesn't, well, I've got a tight schedule to keep."

"Sure, but I think he left this area," Crystal reported.

The girls came over to look at Caleb. "How long have you had him?" one asked.

"Oh, just a few days. He was given to me—a reward actually."

"A reward? No kidding? What did you do?" they quizzed.

"Well, this sounds kind of weird, but we stopped a runaway stagecoach that was carrying a shipment of stolen gold." Crystal watched for their reactions. She'd been tempted to tell a lie, since the truth was hard to tell, and harder to believe. She really didn't want to go into the details.

63

Fortunately, Chad ordered them to gather their trash and load up. She could hear the girls telling the others about what Crystal had said.

Before they climbed in, the boy named Damian yelled, "Mountain momma, you're the woman of my dreams!"

The others shoved him into the raft. He untangled himself and shouted once more, "If you're ever in Chicago, just give me a call."

One of the girls hollered above the roar of the river, "Yeah, he'll be listed under creep!"

They all waved at Crystal, and she waved back.

"Friends of yours?" a voice said close by.

Crystal jumped, and goose bumps ran down her arms and legs.

Shawn and Grady were ten feet behind her.

"Shawn! I didn't hear you coming."

"I guess you were too absorbed with something else." He smiled. "Who were those guys?"

"Oh, just some kids riding the rapids. They weren't here long," she replied.

"And what's that?" he pointed to the beached sack.

"A bag of cement for a guy named Davenport who rented our cabin before we did. I guessed that from what Bucky Switzer told us, and I met this old man, a geologist named Doc Stanton and . . ."

"Hold on, let's talk this out over lunch. Look what I brought." Shawn untied a cloth bag from Grady's back. He loosened his cinch, and Grady joined Caleb.

Crystal and Shawn sat on some flat rocks. "My aunt's quite a cook," Shawn explained. "In this package is fried chicken, here's some homemade biscuits, and over here in the cottage cheese container's some great coleslaw. Even if you never liked coleslaw, you'll like this kind. And here it is— ta da—a whole peach pie!"

Crystal shook her head in amazement. "And it's not even munched. I'm impressed."

"Hey, have I got an aunt, or do I have an aunt?" he chimed in.

The food tasted extra good to Crystal, partly because she was now ravenous, and partly because it was homemade. She told Shawn all about Doc Stanton. Finally she smiled up at him and said, "Hey, we haven't eaten that pie. Show me the plates, and I'll dish it up."

"Plates? All we need are a couple plastic forks. You start on one side, and I'll dig in on the other. Let's see who hits the middle first."

Crystal felt a little uncertain about this arrangement, but she gamely stuck her fork in when Shawn did. Before she'd eaten five bites, Shawn had his half consumed. "I'm full now; why don't you finish it?" she suggested. She didn't need to tell him twice.

As he scraped the pan clean, he said, "I think that will hold me until dinner—next Sunday's dinner."

Crystal saddled Caleb and started back up the trail.

"What about that cement?" Shawn asked.

"The guy that dropped it said just to leave it there."

"We can't let him trash up my river," Shawn asserted.

"Your river?"

"Yes, ma'am. Dad always says that public lands belong to all of us. We should treat them as though we owned them. I sure wouldn't let anyone abandon a sack of cement on my pretty beach. We've got time, why don't we take it on up to Gretchen's?"

"Who is Gretchen?"

"She runs some summer cattle up around the bend in the river. She's got the best little grazing valley around here. It's just a mile or two north.

Crystal was intrigued. "How does she get her cattle in there?"

"She trucks them in by the forest service road to the top of the bluff, then drives them on down to the valley herself. She's quite a lady. She was a championship rider in her day. There're still some trophies at Salmon River High School with her name on them. You'll like her, I think."

Shawn dragged the sack to his horse and struggled to lift the awkward bundle to the back of his saddle. Then as he led the way, they quickly rounded the bend and faced the entrance to a box canyon. A beautiful meadow was fenced off, and a narrow lane ran along the center of it. Far to the back, Crystal could see a log cabin that looked no bigger than the one she and her dad rented.

The meadow still showed green in contrast to the baked, bare mountains directly east. A hand-split rail fence separated the pasture into several sections. As they neared the cabin, Crystal recognized a riding arena, complete with chutes, pens, and even barrels.

A heavyset woman in blue jeans and plaid work shirt, carrying an ax, walked out from behind a small barn. She peered at them. "Shawn Sorensen," she called, "is that you?"

"Hi, Gretchen. This is my friend, Crystal Blake, from California." Shawn dismounted as Gretchen broke out in a wide, friendly grin.

"Well, come on down, honey," she encouraged Crystal, "I don't get many callers. Sure glad to see you."

Crystal slid off Caleb as Shawn chatted, "How's the summer treating you, Gretchen?"

"Not bad. All I've seen is a black bear and an amorous prospector. Nothing I couldn't chase off. What brings you two into the back country?"

"Had a picnic on the beach," Shawn explained. "Some rafter left a sack of unclaimed cement. Wondered if you might take care of it for us. Supposed to go to a man named Davenport. But Crystal thinks he left town a few days ago."

"Just toss it over there by that stump. If no one comes looking for it, I'll make me a new front step. Say, can you stay awhile?"

"I'm afraid not. I want to beat the shadows up

that hill." Shawn turned to Crystal. "I forgot to tell you. Gretchen winters out near our place in Riggins. She never misses any of our football or basketball games."

"You guys ought to take the whole state in basketball this year," she boasted. "If you can just get by the Huskies."

They remounted, and Crystal looked around the arena again. "Do you still ride in rodeos?" she questioned.

"Only in my daydreams. Although I still have a pretty good time running the barrels, my roping's slowed down over the years."

"She's the girls' coach on the rodeo team, too," Shawn informed her. "At least until she moves up to this backcountry for good." Shawn smiled at Gretchen.

Crystal suddenly thought of something. As Shawn waved at Gretchen and started out of the canyon, Crystal held back. "Gretchen," she said when she thought Shawn was out of earshot, "if I come down here tomorrow, would you have time to show me how to do barrel racing? I'm a real new rider, but could you just go over the basics or something?"

"Why sure, honey. You come on down and ask your folks about spending the night. That way would give us two days at it. In fact, they could come, too. I sure don't mind having company now and then."

"Well, thanks. But, I don't know about overnight. In fact, I'm not positive I can come at all. My dad and I are staying at the cabin behind Bucky's Cafe. And since my dad's on a writing project, I'm not sure what his schedule will be."

"I sure hope you can make it. And listen, give Bucky a message for me, will you? Tell him I'm going to have thirty gallons of huckleberries ready for him when I pull out of here. And tell him I won't take less than fifteen dollars a gallon for them."

"Okay, and thanks. I hope to see you tomorrow." Crystal spurred Caleb with the heels of her tennis shoes. She could see Shawn waiting for them up ahead.

The trip uphill was slower and more tedious than the one down. Shawn seemed preoccupied, and Caleb showed no signs of wanting to keep up with the palomino. Crystal viewed a couple young deer scampering away, but little else. She was deep in thought herself, trying to figure out how she'd talk her dad into letting her visit Gretchen tomorrow. She wanted to keep it from Shawn and maybe surprise him later with her newly acquired skills.

The pine trees cast long shadows by the time Crystal and Shawn reached Bucky's pasture. They sped to the cabin. Mr. Blake sat on the porch looking at the clay deed.

"I won't be able to come by tomorrow," Shawn began. "I need to do some things at Granddad's place. But, I could be back the day after. Will you

69

folks still be around?" he asked Mr. Blake.

"We won't be leaving until Friday. But we will have to leave then. Crystal's got school on Monday," Mr. Blake said.

"I'll definitely try to see you before then," Shawn said, and turned for the highway.

Crystal liked the way Shawn had said that last sentence. She thought about it as she busied herself with Caleb's rubdown procedure. After he was safely in the pasture, she returned to her dad. "Busy day, Dad?"

"Mostly just frustrating," he told her. "Nothing but frustrating."

6

GOOD NEWS AND BAD NEWS

CRYSTAL'S DAD WALKED OVER TO THE BED, LAY down on his back, propped up his head, and let out a deep breath. Crystal sat down on a suitcase as she listened.

"Bucky and I were barely off the highway when the road turned to dirt, and we suddenly hit a dirt slide. It looked like half the mountain filled the road. We couldn't veer left because that side dropped off into a creek. To the right was the cliff from which the dirt came. So we backed out.

"Bucky said it was very strange to see a slide like that in the summer. Those usually come during the heavy spring runoff. In June, the crews come in and clean up the back roads. Anyway, he knew another route, but it was rough road and would take longer. But we meant to keep trying. We climbed straight up some hairpin curves with sheer drops on the right, and no room to let another car pass on the left. The potholes and boulders in the roadway were as big as Caleb.

"After two hours of winding the crest of the mountains, we reached the Pine Mill area. We broke out of timberline and headed across a granite pass. The roadway faded completely. I told Bucky I'd be glad to forget the whole thing. But he wanted to press on. Said he could find that mine. And he was right. Minutes later we saw a huge sheet metal building, and a tall stack beside it with a small column of smoke puffing out.

"The problem was, a new, ten-foot-high chain link fence bordered the grounds, the front gate's locked, and the only living thing we could see are two German shepherd guard dogs. They looked like a cross between timber wolves and National Football League linebackers. We hollered to get someone's attention, but no one seemed to be around.

"We finally got Bucky's truck turned around. Then we saw a wind sock. Just like small airports have. We went over to investigate and found a heliport, with just enough crushed gravel to form a pad to land one helicopter.

"We finally bounced our way out of the hills, and Bucky's truck lost a muffler. By the time we got out it was past noon, and we had nothing to show for it but stiff necks and a dirty pickup. Now, I'm hungry for pizza, would you believe?"

"Where would we find pizza?" Crystal asked even as she began to taste the melted cheese and crispy crust.

"Down in Grangeville. It's a bit of a drive, but you said you had a lot to talk bout. Can you be ready in ten minutes?"

"Ten minutes?" she wailed. "Dad, I'm really

grubby. I've been in the rain and the sand and the wind and . . ."

He just smiled and said, "Canadian bacon, green peppers, and extra cheese. . . ."

"That's no fair," she said. "Okay, I'll be ready in ten minutes! But let me warn you," she said as she flew into the next room, "you can't expect perfection in ten minutes." She peeked back out. "If there are any cute boys there, I'll die."

"I thought you already found a cute boy. You know, the blond one, about six feet tall, and what was it? Oh, yes, the one with the 'dreamy eyes.' "

"Well, you never know when a girl needs Plan B," she yelled through the sheet-covered door.

"I'm really impressed with the way you figured out this one plate, Crystal," he said when she returned twelve minutes later.

"What do you think about that missing name?" Crystal asked.

"That does seem a strange coincidence."

"Let's hurry and go. I want to tell you about what I heard from a retired geologist named Doc." She grabbed her denim jacket, and Mr. Blake closed up the cabin.

It was completely dark by the time Crystal finished telling of Caleb's race to the highway and about Doc Stanton, the Final Questers, and Gretchen. By then they had found a place called Fat Maudie's Pizza. Crystal almost asked her dad about going to Gretchen's ranch, then decided to wait until after they ate.

73

They had finished their salads and were waiting for their pizza when Crystal got up her nerve to ask about going to Gretchen's. But he spoke first. "While we have a minute, why don't you use that pay phone to call home?"

"Me?" Crystal responded in surprise.

"Sure, you haven't talked to Mom or Karla in over a week. And be sure to say something to Allyson. She doesn't like being left out. I think I'll have some more salad. Tell them we'll drive long hours, and we aim to arrive Saturday night."

The minute she heard her mother's voice, she recapped the whole week's events rapid-fire. She stopped long enough to greet her two-year-old sister, Allyson, who had a limited, but cheerful, phone vocabulary. Crystal finally paused to ask, "And how are you guys doing?"

"Crystal, is your dad near?" her mother inquired.

"He's at the table. Do you want me to get him?"

"No, but do tell him the contract from Heritage Press came today."

Crystal got excited. "The one he's been working on? The big one?

"That's the one. And the advance is worth more than we ever expected. Tell him if he doesn't get home soon, Karla and I are going to have one great shopping trip. Hug Dad for me, and here's Karla with some news, too."

"Hi, Crys," her sister's familiar voice said.

"Hi, yourself. You won't believe this guy named

74

Shawn I met. And how's cheerleader practice?"

"Who knows?" Karla's voice seemed to fade.

"What do you mean, who knows? You know. You're on the squad," Crystal answered.

"You mean, *was* on the squad. Sherri Martin came back to town Monday. She's going to Citrus Valley after all. She went right in and asked Mr. Cramer if she could have her position back. Since school hadn't started yet, he agreed."

"Where does that leave you?"

"I'm first alternate. I'm only in if one of the girls breaks a leg or something."

"Karla, that isn't fair. They shouldn't go back on their word." Crystal tried to support her sister.

"Wait until you hear the crazy part," Karla continued. "Since I'm no longer a cheerleader, I asked the coach to be reinstated on the volleyball team. He said since I missed the first nine practices, he couldn't let me on. Isn't that like good old Citrus Valley High for you? Always lost in the shuffle."

"Wait until I tell you about the high schools up here. Hey, I've got to go." Crystal saw her dad waving and pointing to his watch. "Talk to you Saturday night, bye."

"You want the good news or the bad news?" Crystal chomped into a slice of pizza full of melted cheese and pepper.

"Give me the bad first, then I'll be free to enjoy the good."

Crystal wiped her mouth with a napkin and reported about Karla.

"How's she taking it?" Mr. Blake said as he pushed away from the table.

"Oh, she can handle it. Of course, she did say something about running away from home and joining a commune." She finished off the pizza before giving him the good news about the book contract.

Mr. Blake leaped to his feet and started across the room.

"Where are you going?" Crystal called out.

"To call your mother."

"I thought you said I talked too long already," she managed to say.

"You did. I didn't," came the reply.

Crystal had never seen her dad more animated. Book contracts always were a cause for celebration, but this one really got him in motion. This was definitely the time to approach the subject of going to Gretchen's.

When Mr. Blake returned, she began, "Dad, I was wondering . . . I've been wanting to ask you something . . . well, you remember that woman, Gretchen, I told you about? She invited me to come visit her tomorrow, even said I could spend the night, and she'd teach me how to do barrel racing. Well, I know it's kind of . . ."

"That just might work out." Mr. Blake seemed to jump at the opportunity.

"I realize I'm only fourteen, but . . . what? Did you say yes?" Crystal came to attention.

"You've got it, kiddo," he encouraged.

76

"But, but, I haven't even got to the begging part yet," she sputtered.

"Spare me," he laughed. "However, I do have three conditions. One, I want to check with Bucky or Shawn's father or someone to get an idea about who this woman is. Two, you're going to have to figure a way to let me know that you made it there safely. And three, you'll have to spend the night and not come back out until Thursday after lunch."

"You're kidding."

"As it turns out, I need to go to Spokane tomorrow and make some contacts. Then, I want to go over to Winchester. I wouldn't be back until Thursday, so if your plans can be worked out, they'll fit with mine."

The next morning the sun peeked through the half-pulled window shade. Crystal found her father working over some papers spread across his bed. "A new book idea?" she asked.

"No, just spending money, maybe," he smiled.

"What's up?"

"It has to be my little secret for just a while longer," he said, then added, "trust me."

"The last time I heard that I ended up with braces for two years," she said, screwing up her face. "How long have you been up? It's only seven."

"Don't ask. I've been down to Bucky's for breakfast. Found out your lady friend is Gretchen Maltby. She was one of the most famous rodeo riders back in the fifties. She did stunts for all the movie stars. Her brother's the state senator from this district. Bucky said a lot of good riders learned their skills down at Gretchen's ranch.

"So I can go for sure?" she blurted.

"Hold on. Bucky also says she has a CB radio with a little portable generator down there that she uses for emergencies. When you get there, have her call Bucky and check in, and let me know for sure if you'll be staying the night. The only thing that bothers me is sending you down that trail alone."

"But, I went down it alone yesterday," she informed him.

"What? I thought Shawn was with you."

"He caught up with me at the river, but the rest of the way I went alone."

"This time go straight to Gretchen's. Don't stop, and don't get off your horse. Okay?"

"Sure, Dad, and thanks. This is really important to me. Know what I mean?" she asked.

"I sure do! Now, go in there and scrub up. I'll wait around to see you get off safely."

Crystal wasn't sure what kind of facilities Gretchen would have. She figured there was no electricity. "How about hot water?" she wondered aloud. She still hadn't gotten to the Laundromat, but this time it didn't matter. All she needed were jeans, a couple T-shirts, and her jacket.

She carried her duffel bag to the other room, where her dad was shoving letters into yellow clay.

78

"I decided that it was impossible to figure these letters out," he exclaimed, "so I just began copying the message you and Shawn put together. Look at this."

"They're identical." Crystal hurried to help him find the final letters.

"But the date's different. It says December 18th, 1905," Mr. Blake pointed out.

Crystal pointed to a pile of unused type. "What are those leftover letters?"

"They could be a name to fit in line two." Her dad spread the letters out.

Crystal snapped her fingers. "Doc Stanton said the professor's name was Clayton. Can you spell Clayton with the letters?"

"I sure can, and look at this. The rest could spell Hiram W. Was that his name?"

"I don't think Mr. Stanton mentioned a first name. Can you decipher what it all means, Dad?"

"No, and I don't know when I'll have time to work on it. Now I've got to head to Spokane. How long do you figure it'll take you to reach Gretchen Maltby's ranch?"

"At least two hours," she replied.

"Okay, I'll call Bucky from Spokane. You try your best to get through to him no later than 11:30. If you don't, I'll bring the entire Idaho National Guard down here to find you. Got it?"

"Yup!" she grinned.

She was well down the creek trail before she remembered she hadn't eaten breakfast.

She pressed on into the beautiful box canyon and headed toward Gretchen's log house. The friendly rancher rode up on a roan Appaloosa that had the sweetest eyes Crystal had ever seen on a horse. "Hey, you made it," Gretchen greeted.

"I need to radio Bucky and let my dad know I'm here," she said first thing.

"You got it, honey." Gretchen glanced at her duffel bag. "You're staying the night, I hope?" Crystal nodded.

Crystal was amazed at the inside of Gretchen's cabin. True, the rooms were small and somewhat dark because of small windows and no electricity, but they held lovely antique furniture, handmade quilts, and bearskin rugs. The cabin had two bedrooms, a large kitchen, a living room, a pantry, and a bathroom. The bathroom consisted of a hand pump for water, a tiny basin, and a large bathtub in the middle of the room.

"All the comforts of home," Gretchen grinned. "Except for the little building out back." She pointed to the outhouse. "You know about those things?"

"Oh sure," Crystal laughed.

Gretchen went to send the message to Bucky. When she returned, Crystal stammered. "When can we start? You know, the barrel racing lessons?"

"I'm ready if you are. You're not too tired of riding?"

"Not a bit. I'm too anxious to learn."

As they walked out to the barn and horses, Crystal asked, "How did you get all that furniture way back in here?"

"My grandfather brought it when he went to work for Pop Wilson back in 1892. Pop had the idea of building a toll road out of the back side of the mines, down to the river at the east side of this canyon. They worked two years to rough out the road. Pop gave my grandfather this canyon meadow if he'd live here and act as agent. He figured the gold shipments could be sent by river from here. Could save ten days off the overland journey."

She opened the barn door and continued. "The first shipment made it down the road just fine, but got dumped in the river by the rapids. Then the mines shut down one after another. So Pop abandoned the project and left for Alaska. My grandfather stayed on and built up the ranch. For years he carried stuff down the old mine road. But it washed out so many times it became unusable. It's been abandoned since the early thirties. She patted Crystal's horse. "What's this fellow's name?"

"He's Caleb, from the Bible," Crystal told her.

"Caleb, sure, the good friend of Joshua. They were the only two scouts who trusted God would give them the promised land. One thing not having any phone, neighbors, or TV does for me, it gives me plenty of time to read the good book."

Crystal started to mount Caleb. "Where do you want us to start?"

"I want Caleb to stay where he is and get some

rest. But you, get out in the arena. This first exercise you can do yourself."

Crystal tried not to show her surprise. She followed Gretchen to the arena. "You see those three barrels? Barrel number 1 is near the right fence; barrel number 2 is by the left fence; and barrel number 3 is at the far end." Gretchen drew a line in the dirt with the heel of her boot. "This line's your starting point. Now, watch this pattern." She sketched with a stick as she talked.

"You'll be running the pattern you'll be riding. First to the left side of barrel 1, cut quickly to the right and circle the barrel. Dash to barrel number 2 to the right side, cut quickly to the left. Almost circle the barrel and dash to the far end to the right side of number 3. Cut quick to the left, then run back here to the finish line. You got that?"

Crystal nodded. "I think so."

"Then go for it."

Crystal ran the first two barrels correctly, but forgot which side to take the far barrel. Gretchen yelled out reminders. Crystal crossed the finish line winded and dusty.

"Okay, great. Now repeat that ten times in a row without a mistake," Gretchen instructed.

Thirty-five minutes later Crystal dragged her aching legs to the barn. She held her side. "Now do we get to ride the barrels?" she prompted.

"Not yet," Gretchen said—much too cheerfully, Crystal thought. "There's something more important. Come on up to the house."

82

PIONEER WOMAN

C RYSTAL HUFFED AND PUFFED TO KEEP STEP WITH her hostess. "What's this important next step?" she gasped.

"Dinner," came the reply. "Unless you'd like to run the barrels some more?" She looked at Crystal, waiting for a response.

Crystal grinned sheepishly. "No thank you. I'm bushed."

"Now remember, that's exactly how Caleb feels sometimes. You let him rest another hour, and he'll give you some good riding this afternoon. Besides, I want to show you how to make elk jerky pie."

"I've never heard of it," Crystal exclaimed.

Gretchen held open the screen door. "You'll love it," she said with confidence.

And Crystal did. The deep-dish potpie was served with stir-fried garden vegetables and wild plum preserves. All were cooked over a wooden stove and served on pink-and-purple flowered china dishes which were slightly chipped. Crystal helped clean up, and then they sat on the porch. Except for the ever-present stirrings of the livestock, they were utterly alone. Crystal couldn't imagine it being any different a hundred years earlier.

"Don't you ever get lonely down here?" she asked.

"Yes," Gretchen answered slowly. "But most times I'm so busy, or everything's so beautiful, I forget to be lonely."

Crystal wondered how personal she dared to get. "Gretchen, you know, it might not be so lonesome if you had someone to share this with. I mean, have you ever been, ever thought of, being married?"

Gretchen sat silent for a moment, and Crystal feared she'd offended her. Then she spoke. "Crystal, how old are you?"

"Fourteen."

"Well, the year I turned sixteen, I decided on the kind of man I would marry someday. He had to ride the rodeo, be tall and thin, be charming yet decisive, tender yet strong. He had to know cattle, love to live in the remote west, have a firm belief in the Lord, be a good listener, and be a lot of fun." Gretchen laughed. "And most of all, he had to be crazy in love with me."

"That sounds pretty good to me," Crystal said, "What happened?"

Gretchen sighed. "Well, I'm fifty-five years old, and I'm still looking. I was searching for a perfect man, and I forgot the good book says no one's perfect. . . . Come on, let's ride!"

They walked to the barn, and Gretchen gave

some instruction. "Take a look at these saddles. This one's considerably lighter than yours. You see, your saddle's made for roping, which is exactly what Caleb's probably used to. But my saddle's for barrel racing. You don't need a big horn to throw a dally on, but you do want a deep bucket so you can cut those corners."

As Crystal prepared Caleb, Gretchen continued. "There's a girl up on the Little Salmon named Terri Biggers. She was going to sell her saddle. Ask Shawn where she lives, and you might get a good deal. Shawn's a good friend of hers."

"How good?" Crystal blurted out before she thought. She wasn't even sure she wanted to know.

"Oh, they did some matched-pairs competition a few years ago. In the parades. She's got blonde hair, just like yours. Except hers is real curly."

Gretchen couldn't have said anything to make Crystal feel more insecure. Suddenly she felt very plain. "Me and my straight hair," she moaned.

Gretchen went right into the main instructions. "Here's what you do. Take Caleb into the arena, run him in circles to the right, getting smaller with every circle. Then run him in left-handed circles, again making them smaller each time."

"Okay, then what?" Crystal prompted.

Gretchen smiled. "Just do that over and over again. I'll watch a minute; then I'll need to ride out and check on the cattle."

Crystal pulled her long hair back and lifted it off her neck in a ponytail. Then she walked Caleb to the arena. He acted excited as they got closer. "That horse has been in arenas before," Gretchen noted. "Probably in roping events. You take good care of him; he's a smart horse. But that's the only kind they raise at A. B. Kirkland's."

"How did you know he came from the Kirkland ranch?" Crystal asked.

"The rocking forty-four brand," she replied, and Crystal blushed that she hadn't thought of that. "A.B. and I got to be really close—thirty years ago," Gretchen hinted.

"How come he wasn't the right one?" Crystal inquired with a sideways glance.

"He wasn't tall and thin. But then, who am I to talk?" She laughed, and motioned Crystal to begin.

Caleb took to the exercises well. He quickly fell into a rhythm, but it seemed to Crystal that he turned easier left, than to the right.

"Keep doing those for about forty-five minutes to an hour, then let him rest," Gretchen hollered. "I should be back by then, and we'll get to those barrels."

As Crystal and Caleb got more used to each other and the routine, Crystal's mind began to wander "Who is this Terri Biggers?" she moped. "What if Shawn's visiting her right now? He said he was going to take care of his grandfather's place, but who knows? Curly blonde hair? Ha! I'll bet she's stuck up. I'm glad I'm not stuck up. I'm not really stuck up, am I, Lord?"

Crystal checked her watch. They'd been circling

for an hour. "One more time each direction, boy," she crooned to Caleb. She encouraged him through two more sets, then rode him to the barn, loosed the cinch, and gave him water and hay.

At the house she washed up and looked for a snack. She grabbed a couple hard biscuits and filled them with wild plum preserves. From the porch she scanned every direction, but couldn't see anything except white-faced cows. She went back into the cabin and noticed a pair of binoculars on a shelf.

She carried the binoculars outside and surveyed the ranch, but she still couldn't see Gretchen. Out of curiosity, she tried to look over the canyon walls. With the help of the 10X glasses, she examined the gullies, rocks, and trees along the rim. The faint outlines of what could be the old grade caught her eye. "Maybe that's the way to the abandoned mine Gretchen told me about," she theorized.

Crystal replaced the binoculars and walked out to the barn. Just as she reached Caleb, Gretchen rode up. "Ready for the barrels?" she challenged.

"I sure am," Crystal said with enthusiasm.

"Mount up and follow me," Gretchen directed.

At the arena, Gretchen dismounted and drew another thick line in the dirt. "Remember the pattern you ran this morning? Now I want you to do the same thing with Caleb. Only, listen up real careful. Ride him up to the line, and just sit a few minutes. Get him in the habit of waiting for your command. Then, cut him to the right and circle him around once before you ever cross the line. Hit that line running. Run him in the exact pattern I told you. You do remember, don't you?"

Crystal nodded.

"Okay," she continued, "race back across the finish line, but don't let him stop. Cool him down by walking him several right-hand circles. Then, walk him back up to the line and make him stand still.

"Repeat the process, only this time walk him through the whole routine, exactly as I said. You ready?"

"I think so," Crystal responded.

"You can do it," Gretchen encouraged. "You've got horse sense. I've been on a horse since I was two, and I've seen hundreds of riders. Folks seem to be born with horse sense, or not. You've got it. You just need the experience to learn the skills."

"You really think so?" Crystal beamed in delight.

"No doubt about it. Now, I want you to watch me do the barrels. And time my run."

"From line to line?" Crystal inquired.

"That's right." Gretchen took off faster than Crystal could look down. She circled the first, second, and final barrel, tore back to the finish line, circled her horse a few times, then led him back to the starting line. He stood still as she asked, "Well, how'd I do?"

"I think it was right at nineteen seconds, maybe a little under. You caught me off guard," Crystal admitted. "What's a good time?"

"For high school rodeo—probably around eighteen seconds. But to win the nationals you've got to be in the sixteens. I had a 16.6 many years ago."

"How fast do the girls on your team go? Say someone like . . ."

"Like Terri Biggers?" Gretchen finished.

Crystal nodded. "Just for an example."

"Terri doesn't ride barrels. She's too busy with horse shows. The others all ride in the eighteens and nineteens."

Gretchen rode to the gate and dismounted. She climbed the top rail of the fence, took off her worn straw hat, and signaled Crystal to begin.

Caleb responded obediently to Crystal's commands. He waited, circled right, then started across the line. Crystal made all the turns in the right direction, then hustled him across the finish. She ran him in slowing circles and stopped him. Caleb urged her to race him again. She had to hold his reins tight to keep him still.

"That's great," Gretchen called.

Crystal and Caleb repeated the pattern over and over again. Gretchen yelled encouragement and correction from her perch on the fence rail.

As Crystal and Caleb waited a moment between runs, Gretchen hopped down and walked over. "Crystal, you need to swing a little wider on the first pass by the barrel, then cut him tight against it as you come around. Give him room at first as you're flying by, but as you slow for the turn, cut it closer and tear off for that next barrel."

As Crystal nudged Caleb to the line, Gretchen added, "You want me to time you after you walk him through?"

Crystal's stomach churned, but she said, "Sure." She walked Caleb around the course and returned.

Crystal made a couple right circles and hit Caleb for full stride. Caleb made a good first run and picked up speed for the second barrel. But Crystal cut it too tight and had to swing wide around the second barrel. Caleb had a good stride as they approached the last barrel, but they came too close to the backside and Crystal hit her ankle against the barrel. She winced as she spurred Caleb on across the finish line.

"How'd I do?" she cried through the pain.

"Keep him winding down," Gretchen reminded her.

Crystal guided Caleb to the line, and rested him.

"You had a great finish time. Right at twenty-four seconds," Gretchen informed her.

"Twenty-four? Is that all?" Crystal complained.

"Don't you be getting all bothered about times yet," Gretchen scolded. "This is day one. Remember? Hey, did you hurt yourself?" she asked as Crystal rubbed her ankle against the horsehide.

"Oh, I banged myself, but not too bad," Crystal assured her as she reached down to massage her foot.

"Well, how about the rest of you? Are you saddle broke yet?" Gretchen prompted.

"I think so. Anyway, I feel just fine." Crystal raced Caleb through four more runs, walking him in between. Gretchen timed each one: one twenty-three and three twenty-fours.

When they rode back to the barn, Crystal stood in the stirrups and swung her sore right foot over the saddle, determined to hit the ground like a seasoned rider. She turned to speak to Gretchen, and collapsed right on her face.

She looked up in embarrassment. "Sometimes I have a tough time getting off."

Gretchen helped her up. "It could be your ankle," she suggested.

"I don't think so," Crystal said. "It's just like both legs are asleep. You know what I mean?"

"Sure do. I won a one-hundred-mile endurance race once and couldn't move for three days," she chuckled. "Try to walk it off slowly, get your circulation going again. I'll take care of Caleb's saddle."

As they headed to the cabin, Crystal looked at her watch. It was just 5:15, but already the sun had set in the west because of the high ridge on that side of the canyon. The peacefulness of it all poured into Crystal's tired body. She thought about home, about the crowded cul-de-sac in the midst of thousands of people. She thought about the freeways that were jammed bumper to bumper with restless, rude drivers. She thought about locks on doors and windows and life that revolved around television shows and shopping malls.

Gretchen interrupted Crystal's reverie. "Now

you know why I come back year after year."

"I really appreciate your letting me come," Crystal remembered to say. "We'll be going back home day after tomorrow."

"Friday? Are you leaving in the morning or evening?" Gretchen asked.

"I don't know yet, but why does it matter?"

"The junior rodeo at Nez Perce is this weekend." Gretchen winked at Crystal. "Could be a good time to show your friend Shawn what you know."

"A rodeo?" Crystal gasped. "I couldn't possibly be ready for that—could I?"

"Well, I doubt you'd win any silver, but you can't get enough competition," Gretchen explained. "I don't think I'm ready to have anybody see me," Crystal replied. "I'd be too scared."

"Think about it. But right now, let's get some supper," Gretchen said, as she held the door open for Crystal.

Supper consisted of hot roast beef sandwiches, fresh milk, and baked apples. After her second baked apple, Crystal heard Gretchen moan.

"It's that pesky tooth again. I've been babying it for two months. I keep thinking I'll last six or eight more weeks and take care of it later. Dentists and doctors, that's what you miss most of civilization down here. There, it's eased up. At least it makes for a pretty good appetite represser."

It was nearly dark when they finished cleaning up the kitchen. Gretchen lit a kerosene lantern and walked to the front porch. "Any house that doesn't have a porch to sit on, isn't really a home," she philosophized. Crystal had to agree as the cool air revived her.

Crystal had planned a sponge bath, but Gretchen insisted that she try the big tub. She heated water on the wood stove, and sprinkled some bubble bath in the tub. "It's a luxury down here," Gretchen admitted, "but I like to spoil myself on some things."

Crystal sank deep into the warm water and bubbles. Not only was the tub the largest she'd ever been in, but it was the first she'd seen with eagle's claws surrounding brass balls for legs.

If the bath was a treat, the bed was pure delight. The tiny guest room was engulfed by a feather mattress almost as tall as Crystal. When she climbed up into it, she speculated whether it would swallow her alive. After a few moments' adjustment, she proclaimed it the softest mattress in the world. The hours of riding, combined with the hot meal and soothing bath, took their toll on her. She meant to review what she'd learned about barrel racing, but the next thing she knew daylight had broken and Gretchen was standing beside her.

"Crystal," she whispered, "I'm sorry to wake you so rudely. I'm afraid I'll have to be a poor hostess. This sore tooth has kept me awake all night. I've just got to get up top and get to a dentist."

Crystal sat up and rubbed her eyes. "Would you like me to go with you?" she said, with obvious disappointment.

"You don't have to. You're welcome to stay here. Maybe after you fix yourself some breakfast, you could saddle up Caleb and ride the ranch for me. All that means is pumping those four water troughs full, checking the gates, and seeing that no fences are down. Doesn't take me an hour. If I hurry, I can make it up to Elk City and back by one o'clock. If you need to leave before then, just close the gate as you go. And of course, you can run patterns around the barrels." Gretchen tried to smile as she hurried out.

Crystal literally had to pluck herself out of the bed. As she settled in the kitchen, she felt like a true pioneer woman. She found some homemade bread, more wild plum preserves, some cold milk, and elk jerky. The jerky tasted so good, she stuck extra pieces in her jeans pocket.

She marched out to the front porch, took a deep breath, and said aloud in her most dramatic voice, "Well, I reckon I'd best mosey on out to the barn, instead of jist standing here burning daylight."

Caleb was as noncommittal in his attitude as ever. He casually observed Crystal as she prepared to ride. They headed around the ranch, starting with the front lane. Then they covered the west wall, which had the most daylight peeking over the eastern mountains. Crystal pumped the four troughs and could see no problems with the gates or fences. She was relieved, because she didn't know what she'd do if she did see anything wrong.

By the time she reached the east wall, she considered her duty done. But she heard a calf bellow somewhere up the side of the canyon, not far from the fence. She crossed over a dry creek bed, rode behind a couple of downed cottonwood trees, and discovered the beginning of a trail. That's when she recalled the old mine road Gretchen told her about, that she'd seen with the binoculars.

Gretchen mentioned it didn't reach the top anymore, but it sounded as though the calf cried from that direction. She found him standing in the weed-covered abandoned roadway, calling for his mother who bellowed back from the pasture. Crystal wondered what to do now.

Caleb sped into action instead. He began to drive the lost animal back down the grade, toward the pasture. If the calf attempted to move to one side or the other, Caleb cut him off, and he kept moving straight ahead.

At the bottom Crystal opened the gate, and shooed the calf towards its mother. "So, that's how it's done! Good work, Caleb," she complimented. Caleb looked at her with his usual blank expression.

Crystal couldn't believe the time. It was only 7:00 a.m. She'd been up and working for over and hour. The extra time tempted her. She'd like to ride that old road to see how far it went. "I'll bet I'd sure get some grand overview of Gretchen's ranch," she told Caleb.

The roadway proved a mess. In its prime it couldn't have been more than eight feet wide. After years of erosion, Crystal barely found two feet of space. Logs and boulders crisscrossed the trail. Ravines dipped down and across. But, as they climbed, the scene below grew incredible. She could not only see the entire ranch, but rows of loftier mountains beyond. She determined to travel as far as Caleb could go. When he couldn't climb any longer, they'd turn around.

She didn't mention this plan to Caleb, and he forged through everything. A time or two she crouched low in the saddle to duck under limbs and snags. Three-fourths of the way up she saw a seemingly impassable obstacle. A creek had cut across the road and into a sharp canyon wall, leaving a channel six feet wide and about ten feet deep.

Crystal sighed, took one last view of the expansive Idaho panorama, and tried to turn Caleb around. He took several steps down, then abruptly turned to face uphill.

"What's the matter, Caleb?" Crystal called. "You can't get across that ravine." She kicked him hard, and again tried to turn him. He galloped straight up to the washout with Crystal screaming her lungs out. Caleb ignored her and leaped the gorge as if it were a small pasture mud puddle.

When Crystal caught her breath, the terrifying thought hit her: how would they get back? But there was nothing to do but keep going. The trail disappeared sometimes in the soft, slippery soil of the cliffside, but a portion always appeared out ahead.

As they approached the top, Crystal noticed the pine forest that had grown thick and wild since the road had last been level. She couldn't ride Caleb through it or even walk with him. Off to the right, in a sandstone cliff about eight feet high, she discovered crude steps that had been cut into the side. Crystal dismounted.

The steps appeared recently gouged. She turned to Caleb, "You wait for me here. I want to see what's up there before we turn back."

Hand over hand she climbed up the bluff. When she reached the top, she straightened up and brushed herself off. As she ate a piece of jerky, she surveyed the mountain valley she'd entered from the backside.

"Another fantastic backwoods setting," she announced to the atmosphere, "blue skies, green trees, clean air, and a smokestack." Crystal about choked on her jerky. "A smokestack?"

8
THE DARK TUNNEL

F IT HADN'T BEEN FOR THE WISPY COLUMN OF SMOKE, Crystal would never have seen the smokestack. She hiked through the trees in its direction. At the edge of the stand, she realized the smokestack was farther away than she guessed. What she thought was a valley turned out to be a high mountain swale in an otherwise treeless area of the slopes.

From the crest she stood on, Crystal spied the backside of an old mining operation. Sheet metal buildings leaned into the hill beside a factory building with the tall smokestack.

The grounds were enclosed by chain link fence, and to the right, an open area. "Looks like a parking lot, or . . ." Crystal pondered, "or a place to park a helicopter!" She could see a light blue helicopter parked nearby. "This is the Pine Mill mine Dad visited!" she exclaimed.

After a brief survey of the countryside, she turned back toward Caleb. As she brushed through the trees again, a wooden box next to a pile of rocks arrested her attention. She examined it and found a heavy Winchester rifle and ammunition. Some

98

sort of cave opening gaped next to it. Another box held a foot-long, heavy duty flashlight. A couple packages of extra batteries were also in the box.

Crystal flipped on the flashlight and pointed it into the cave. "It's a tunnel! Or mine shaft!" she said under her breath. She remembered her dad telling her the area was honeycombed with old mine shafts. "Too bad he didn't find this one. It even comes with its own light. Maybe I'll just take a quick look around, so I can tell him what it's like," she reasoned.

She only wanted to go in a few feet, where she could still see the opening. Crystal flashed the beam everywhere, but she didn't know what to look for. Nothing here looked like silver or gold. "That's enough of that." She turned to retreat, but something reflected from the light. "Maybe there's silver in here," she said.

She found a pile of tools stashed in a corner: A hammer, a handsaw, pliers, and assorted instruments. They looked in good condition. Crystal held up the saw. A price tag and the name High Mountain Hardware, Elk City, Idaho, hung from it. "That's across the street from Bucky's," she remembered.

A few feet farther someone had stacked wire and boards. "I'll just walk in twenty-five more steps," Crystal decided. But at twenty-five steps, she could see nothing, so she compromised on twenty-five more. That would be the absolute limit. "Besides," she reminded herself, "Caleb's waiting, I'm supposed to watch Gretchen's ranch, and I want to go barrel riding."

She turned the corner of a descending section of the tunnel and spotted a flickering light far down the rocky vent.

Crystal halted and prepared to make a fast exit. As she did, faint voices filtered up to her. She took a cautious step forward. Fifty steps later she recognized the words spoken. The light reflected over the top of some sort of barricade built up in the tunnel. Crystal could see wooden braces, chicken wire, and maybe plaster or cement. She immediately thought of the cement sack they had hauled to Gretchen's. "It's like a false front set at Disneyland or Universal Studios," she thought.

She sat down to listen. Several persons spoke, then were quiet as one man spoke, "I admit, it's one of the craziest things I've seen. As I told you in the helicopter, I've had these old gold-mine stocks for years. My grandfather bought them from a man named Clayton back in 1908. They've been in the family since. But we never knew what to do with them. A few years ago I decided that with gold prices the way they were, I should look into the family claim.

"Early this June I determined to take a break and spend time looking the claims over. Since the Pine Mill was the biggest, I started here. I found Hank to be my guide. He'd worked this shaft in the thirties. Tell them about it, Hank."

The new voice cracked with age. "Yep, old man

Dempsey came in here in the fall of '38. Most of us were half starved and would do anything for room and board. We started cleaning up shafts, and some who could weld fixed up the stamping mill down below. We'd work a few months, then they'd run out of money so we'd go out and make some firewood. They'd hire us again, then lay us off. Anyways, we never got to the gold. All we succeeded in doing was getting it ready. The war come, and we went to the Pacific. Nobody ever did anything more about the gold until Mr. Davenport here."

"Davenport!" Crystal almost said out loud. "That's the name of the man who stayed in our cabin and brought mail to Doc Stanton. The same man who ordered cement!"

Hank kept speaking. "Early in June Mr. Davenport came and asked me to help him open the mine up for inspection. I live down the road a piece, the only cabin in these mountains, and I had nothing better to do, so we put up the fence and cleaned out these shafts. When we reached this one, she'd been plugged up by a cave-in something fierce. Some of them rocks was twice as big as we were. As you can see, most of the beams had to be replaced. I'll never forget the day we broke into this section. We danced around the room for an hour."

Mr. Davenport broke in. "This final cave-in, which we haven't even begun to dig out, must have happened after the shaft had been sealed by the others. See how that mother lode above you runs

101

right into the north slope? They're just starting to get big where they disappear back into the mountains. The main section's still out of sight. It's an incredible find."

A new voice joined the conversation. "Davenport, I appreciate the breakfast, helicopter ride, and the mine tour, but with that much gold, why do you need us?"

"Gentlemen, I need a temporary loan. Or if you're interested, some limited partners. I grubbed out the purest nuggets I could from the stuff that fell down here. Hank and I melted it down into rough gold buttons and sent it off to Denver to be tested."

"Actually, Mr. Davenport, I was up to Calgary that week," Hank interjected.

"Oh, that's right, you were. Anyway, we've been trying to keep the whole thing secret. It's essential that you all keep your mouths shut, too. You see, my biggest fight right now is to establish the mineral rights. There's been some question—I don't have any doubts, but you know the courts. Something like this could be tied up for years. By the time it goes public I want the legalities sewed up."

"Just for fun, what exactly do you expect of us?" a man with a deep voice asked.

"Well, men, I'd like to borrow $100,000 from each of you."

"That's a half million dollars, man! Are you crazy?" another man exclaimed.

"Half of that will go for attorney's fees easy.

Gentlemen, I want to keep everything on the up-and-up, and stay one step ahead of claim jumpers."

"What's the rest of the money for?" the deep voice asked.

"I'll need an extensive security system, and some preliminary repairs on the stamping mill. Right now my only security's the two guard dogs and Hank. And that won't stand against two thousand weekend prospectors. Time's short. I have good reason to suspect that some word's leaked out already. Just last weekend someone tried to rob the armored car that was carrying my gold buttons to Denver. Fortunately, someone discovered the plot and foiled them."

"That's me!" Crystal hissed. "That was the gold down at the rodeo!"

The deep-voiced man wanted to know, "What will we get out of this?"

"I'll return your $100,000 in six months, plus $20,000 interest. Or, if you want . . ."

"Yeah?" someone prompted.

"I'd be willing to take you in as partners. I've got one thousand shares of the Wildflower Mountain Mining Company stock. That's all that was ever issued. I'll give you each ninety-five shares, and keep five hundred myself."

"What happens to the other fifty?"

"They go to Hank," Davenport reported.

"Well, Davenport," the deep-voiced man began, "if all I wanted was $20,000 for my hundred grand, I'd leave it in the bank. Or buy real estate short term. To convince any of us to go in with you, you'll have to give up some of those shares. If, and that's a big if, you want me in on the deal, you'd better offer 150 shares each. That leaves you with two hundred, and Hank with fifty. It also gives us controlling interest. After all, it seems you want us to take all the risk."

"That's not true. I just sold my house on Mercer Island for $95,000. Gentlemen, that's the total sum I could raise. I can't give you controlling interest."

"Just how rich do you want to be? Don't you think there's more than plenty for all of us?" the deep voice answered.

"Oh, sure. It's just the fact that it's mine. Besides, those certificates are good for other claims, not just the Pine Mill," Davenport explained.

"That's the breaks. You take your chances, and we take ours," the spokesman replied.

"Okay, but listen. If I agree to this, you've got to promise to keep it quiet until I say so, right?"

One of the men laughed. "Makes sense to me. We're used to that, aren't we, men? I think I could find myself some unattached investment money somewhere." The others mumbled agreement.

The man called Sidney said, "Davenport, you get us the sample analysis from Denver, then give us a call. Then we'll get together and make some kind of decision. Does that sound right, boys?"

"Okay, okay, but," Davenport replied, "on one condition—you won't mind my contacting other potential investors in the meantime?"

"What other investors?" someone growled.

"I'm a man under pressure. If that report hits the newspapers as public domain, I'm tied to the courts for years. I've got just two weeks before the final analysis. If I can find men willing to invest the money, I'll go with them. Besides, someone else might not demand so many shares," Davenport concluded.

"Listen, Davenport, you led us to believe you were giving us first option," the deep voice said.

Then Sidney intruded, "I'll make you a deal. We come up with fifty percent of the money right away, today if you want, and the other fifty percent after the analysis."

"You guys play it tough," Davenport conceded.

"You aren't dealing with some rank amateurs," one of them boasted.

"I can see that." Davenport paused. "Well, okay, but I somehow feel I'm trading a quarter for two nickels."

Sidney polled the group. "You fellas in on this?"

Crystal could hear them agreeing to return to Spokane by air and come back by 5:00 p.m. that day. Then the mine got dark as the voices began to fade away.

Crystal grabbed the flashlight and panicked a moment when the beam wouldn't go on. She banged it on a rock, and the bright light shone ahead of her. She carefully walked out of the tunnel. It was much steeper going out than entering.

She found the cave entrance and climbed the

rock to get out. The late morning sun blinded her briefly, and she covered her eyes. As she heard the whir of the helicopter overhead, she ducked back into the cave until it was out of sight. Stepping back out, she put the flashlight back in its box and sat down on the rocks.

She looked back down at the mine. "This shaft goes all the way through, so why would anyone go to the trouble to build a barricade? And if it's a hoax, where did that gold on the stage come from? I wonder if Davenport's trying to swindle those men."

She ascended the cliff, then stepped down to where Caleb stoically stood waiting. "Caleb!" she shouted. "We've got to get out of here. Let's get to Gretchen's and try to get a hold of Dad, or somebody. Come on, boy."

She kicked him, but he wasn't to be hurried. Crystal's mind mulled over a hundred plots of intrigue as Caleb slowly picked his way downward. Finally they reached the steep granite wash that he leaped earlier. As Crystal suspected, the jump was impossible on the descending side. There was no space to make a running jump.

Caleb peered over the edge as Crystal got off and looked for a crossing. She found one that a human might manage, but not a horse. Then she saw the tons of loose rocks above the wash. "If I could roll enough of them down, Caleb could cross," she decided.

Crystal led Caleb up the trail a ways, loosened

his cinch, and tied him to a lightning-burned tree trunk. She climbed above the wash and began kicking rocks into the ravine. She hoped to start a rockslide and fill the dry creek bed. But all she managed to do was scrape her sore ankle. "It'll take three days this way."

"Lord," she prayed, "there must be a way."

She hiked up behind a large granite boulder and leaned on it to catch her breath. Suddenly, the huge rock gave way and slid down the hill pushing everything ahead of it into the ravine. Crystal slipped down with it until she rolled and caught herself on a prickly bush. When the dust cleared, the washout was almost filled, just lacking two feet from the roadway. Crystal rushed back to get Caleb.

She led him to the new crossing. "This is the best I can do," she told him. "I know the rocks are slippery and the path's not very wide, but you're a good horse. I know you can do it. See? See how nice it is? Now watch me walk over, then you come right along."

The big gray Appaloosa gazed at the rocky crossing, then slowly stepped over to the other side. "All right!" Crystal shouted with much relief. She remounted, and on they went.

By the time they reached the canyon floor Crystal perspired through her clothes. She turned Caleb into Gretchen's pasture lane. Caleb sprinted off towards Gretchen's house.

Gretchen wasn't anywhere around. Crystal

buzzed through the cabin to the back room. She glanced at the mirror as she whizzed by. She didn't know whether to laugh or cry. Her hair looked like a blonde mop. Her face was mud streaked and smeared. "I'm glad I didn't wear my new hat and ruin it," she consoled herself. "As soon as I reach Bucky's, I'll clean up."

The generator had a motor like their lawn mower back home. she tried to remember how it worked. Crystal yanked on the rope starter. The motor turned over, but didn't start. She pulled and pulled and pulled. Exhausted, she wound the rope one more time and tugged with all her might. This time the motor rattled to life.

Crystal walked over to the radio and flipped the "on" button. She picked up the mike and held down the red switch. "This is Crystal Blake at Gretchen Maltby's," she announced. "I need to talk to Bucky Switzer, and I don't know how to use this radio."

She released the switch and heard static, but nothing else. "I said, hello out there. This is Crystal. Bucky, are you there?"

Still no response.

"Hello! Hello! This is Crystal. Can anybody hear me?"

"Hey, hey, Crystal, Big Jim here, where you calling from?"

Crystal excitedly answered the radio operator. "Big Jim, this is Crystal Blake. Do you know Bucky?"

"Bucky who?" came the reply.

"The one who has the cafe," Crystal explained.

"Which cafe?"

"The one in Elk City," she said, exasperated.

"What part of the country are you in?"

"Elk City, Idaho, where are you?" Crystal snapped.

"Well, Crystal darling, I want you to know you've made my day. I've never talked to anyone that far before. This is Big Jim calling from Silver City, New Mexico."

"I don't want to talk to you," Crystal cried, "I've got to reach Bucky."

"Well," Big Jim howled, "just bake him a pie. It's the quickest way to a man's heart."

Crystal slammed down the radio and shut off the generator. She glanced at her watch: almost noon. "Maybe if I hurry up the trail, I can find somebody." She ran out to Caleb and mounted.

Caleb trotted the stretch out of the box canyon and onto the sandy beach of the river. They began the ascent back to the cabin. All the time her mind raced. "Something tells me those men are going to lose a lot of money, but I'm not positive. Then they'd get the mining stock. However, if the gold's phony—which I can't be sure it is—the certificates . . . Hey, the press! We've got the press! If he printed up new certificates, I could prove it if I showed them the press and plates! It could expose this Davenport—I think."

They continued to plod up the hill. It was 2:00

109

when Caleb edged the forest behind Bucky's meadow. Crystal rode him hard around to the cabin. She jumped down and grabbed the sack and scooped up the press and plates. She scratched out a message for her dad and headed for Bucky's. She ran up the dirt drive, giving Caleb a chance to rest.

"Is Bucky here?" she panted to the waitress.

"Bucky's down at Orofino, won't be back until after supper."

Crystal thanked her and looked up and down the street hoping to see her dad somewhere. "I thought he was supposed to be back by now," she said to no one. "Lord, I'm not really sure what I'm doing, or if there's really anything to do." Then she thought of a poster her dad had in his office back home. It read, "I must do those things in life I would regret not doing."

"That's it," she cried. "I'd really regret not making sure that deal I overheard's not a con." She prayed again as she hustled back to Caleb. "Lord, please give me and Caleb the strength to make it up to that mine one more time."

She tied the press to the back of Caleb's saddle and mounted. The narrow trail was by now very familiar to both of them. They made good time. As they darted out from some fir trees in the clearing. "Gretchen! Gretchen!" she screamed.

"Crystal, is that you? We're down by the creek."

She soon saw Gretchen walking quickly toward her. At Gretchen's side was Doc Stanton. "Gretchen, Mr. Stanton, am I ever glad to see you! Some-

110

thing's going on up at the Pine Mill mine." Crystal reviewed all she'd done and heard. They asked a number of rapid-fire questions, then decided to come along with Crystal. "But we'll have to ride double until we get to the ranch," Gretchen said.

"Maybe I'd better keep going, and you guys catch up," Crystal suggested. "I'd sure hate to get there too late."

"I guess that's best," Gretchen conceded, "but you be very careful. We have no idea what we're up against. Don't put yourself into any kind of jeopardy. Promise?"

Crystal nodded and said, "Gretchen, while you're at the ranch, could you radio Bucky? I'm not sure Dad will see my note, or even understand it, if he does."

As Crystal and Caleb rode by the bend of the river she a saw white water raft on the rapids. But she didn't even bother to wave. Caleb veered to the east side of the canyon and once more began to conquer the old mine road. This time Crystal rode him across her improvised washout crossing.

At ten minutes after five, she reached the top. Her legs wobbled beneath her when she climbed off Caleb. She leaned against him until she got her land legs, then hiked up the steps, through the pine forest, and out to the mine overlook. "The helicopter's here!" Crystal's heart sank.

She headed for the nearest gate in the chain link fence. As she expected, the gate was tightly locked. She attempted to climb it until she heard the dogs.

Then she realized she'd left the press and plates on Caleb's saddle. Even in her anger with herself, she knew she had to go back and get them.

Crystal ran back up the hill to the trees and canyon edge. She stared in amazement to see Caleb standing by a blue spruce. "Caleb! How in the world did you get up here?"

He gave no clue, just stared in the direction of the setting sun. She grabbed the sack, tied up Caleb, and headed for the dark tunnel. Once again she borrowed the flashlight and approached the dank, inky blackness. "I hope these batteries are good," she whispered.

As she neared the barricade she noticed a light and voices. She switched her light off and sat very quietly.

"I hope you don't mind, Davenport," a male voice said, "but we need this test before we turn over our money."

"Of course not, help yourself," came the now-familiar voice. "Will this sample do, or would you rather chip one off yourself?"

"That one will do. You see, this chemical test will show if this is truly gold, and how pure it is. It's not perfect, but it does give us an indication. We've got to protect ourselves," he persisted.

"Hey, in there! I've got to talk to you!" Crystal shocked herself as the echo from her voice bounced along the tunnel shaft.

9
MINE, ALL MINE

WHAT'S GOING ON?" "WHO IS THAT ?" "WHERE are you?" "Sounds like a girl."

A flurry of noisy confusion escaped from behind the barricade. Finally Davenport shouted above the rest. "Where are you?"

The other men quieted down to hear her response. "I'm up the tunnel, behind this plaster and cement. See the small crack at the top? That's my flashlight beam. I'm up here."

"My word! A child's stuck up there. We've got to get her out, Davenport!"

"Shhh!" said Davenport sharply. "Who are you, and how in the world did you get up there?"

"I'm Crystal LuAnne Blake, and this tunnel leads to the top of the mountain. I found it while horseback riding."

"Are you all right?" one of the men called.

"I'm all right, I just need to talk to you. It's important," she hollered.

"Well, just come down," Davenport challenged.

"I can't. There's nowhere to climb. It's all wires and plaster back here, and the little hole's not big enough," she reported.

"Davenport, what does she mean about wire and plaster?" the man called Sidney demanded.

"I have no idea, gentlemen, but I will surely find out. You can certainly see the urgent need we have for security. Imagine a back entrance into this place? And how many more are there?" He called back to Crystal. "We'll meet you around at the gate. Go back to where you got in. Hurry."

"Okay," Crystal shouted, "but it'll take me a few minutes." She hurried up the tunnel to daylight. As she paused at the shaft entrance, she allowed her eyes to adjust, then mounted Caleb and rode him down to the fence. She expected to see all the men. Instead, just one stood there. He wore a dark brown leather jacket, jeans, and hiking boots.

The man opened the gate and motioned Crystal inside. "Now, young lady, what is it you want?"

"Where are the other men?" she asked. "I wanted to talk to all of you."

"The others are still in the mine. Why don't we go join them?" He led Crystal into one of the large buildings that slanted into the mountainside.

"Where's the mine?" she inquired.

"You've seen plenty of it already. Allow me to now show you the toolroom." The man shoved Crystal into a small room filled with dusty shelves. He slammed and bolted the door behind her. A tiny window about six feet up allowed just enough light for Crystal to see. She banged on the door with all her might and screamed.

She stopped in frustration. "They'll never hear

me from here. Now look what I've done. Gretchen told me to wait for them, to not get myself into trouble. Why didn't I keep my mouth shut?"

She searched all over for some way of escape. All she found was a six-foot long piece of channel iron. Though it was heavy, she was able to drag it over to the door. With some effort she succeeded in wedging the iron bar between the door and door-jamb. She hoped to break the lock, using the bar for a pry.

The lock refused to budge, but with a loud crack and crash like cymbals, the bottom of the doorframe broke, and a corner of it bent out.

Crystal crouched on her hands and knees and wiggled through the opening. She found her way back out to the yard and across to the gate. She wanted to get the plates and press from where she'd left them on Caleb's saddle. Halfway across the yard she heard a bone-tingling growl. Two wildly barking, large dogs pursued her.

"Jump, Crystal! Jump!" She swung her head in the direction of the commands. Gretchen and Doc stood next to Caleb on the other side of the locked gate. She made a running leap for the gate and grasped the top with the yapping dogs right be-hind. She made it over in time, but scratched her arms in the attempt. She hit the ground and fell to her knees.

Gretchen came to her aid. "Are you all right?"

Crystal stood to her feet. "I think so. Just some scratches." She explained what had happened.

"How in the world did you get Caleb up that cliff?" Doc wanted to know.

"I didn't. He just followed me somehow. I hope there's another way out, because I'm sure not going to ride him down it. Meanwhile, we've got to get in that mine."

"Hey, what's going on up there?" They all turned to see an old-timer walking down the roadway towards them. "This is private property, you folks can't . . . Gretchen? I didn't know it was you." The man pulled off his hat revealing a shock of white hair.

"Hank, what's going on at the Pine Mill?" Gretchen got right to the point.

Hank told her pretty much what Crystal heard before, then asked, "And who are these two?"

"This is Crystal, a young friend and pupil of mine, and this is Howard Stanton. He spends the summers in the old Wisener place up Badger Draw." Gretchen got back to the subject. "Do you trust this Davenport? Do you really believe there's a new vein?"

"I was right there the day he discovered it. He's even going to give me fifty shares of the stock. I figured I can finally have enough money to move to town," Hank reported. "I just check the gates and feed the dogs every day."

"Hank," Crystal began, "it may be that everything's not as it seems in there. I need to go talk to Mr. Davenport and those men with him. Do you suppose you could feed the dogs while we slip in?"

116

Doc Stanton added, "I'm a geologist. Perhaps I could be of some assistance to all of them."

"Well, now, you may be right, Stanton. They were all complaining in there about how it'd take two weeks to get tests back from the assay office." Hank opened the gate.

"Thanks, Hank," Gretchen said as she led the way in. "Next time you come down fishing, stop by for some huckleberry pie."

"I think maybe I'll buy me a whole bakery," Hank laughed as he lured the dogs out of sight.

At the mine, Doc Stanton announced, "I've spent most my life poking around mountains like this one. You get to where you know just what to expect."

They followed a weak-bulbed electrical cord that plunged back into the mountain. Soon they heard voices and saw bright lights. Doc motioned them all to stand still. This time Crystal could see all the men. The investors wore business suits, with jackets hanging over their arms and ties loosened.

"Like I told you before, men, she overheard us talking about gold and thought she should have a few shares herself just to keep quiet," Davenport lied. "A real brazen kid."

"What did you tell her exactly?" one of them prompted.

"I told her to wait up top, and we'd settle it later. I tell you, men, gold fever . . . "

Crystal stepped out of the shadows, followed by Gretchen and Doc Stanton. "That's not true," she

117

retorted. "He locked me in a room because he was afraid of something I'd say."

"What the—Davenport, what's going on? Do we have a whole family in on this?"

Davenport raised his voice. "Okay, I've had it. I don't know who you people are, but you're trespassing on private property. If you aren't off here in ten minutes, I'll have you arrested. Young lady, I warned . . ."

"You locked me up, and you know it. Men, I don't know who you are, or all that's going on, but look at this. In this sack I have an old printing press with plates for the original mineral rights, and another new plate which—I believe—was forged by this man, Davenport, to establish himself as owner of this mine."

Crystal opened the sack. "Oh, no," she cried. In the long, hard trip down the canyon and back, the clay had dried out and broken up. The pieces lay scattered on the mine floor. Crystal was almost in tears. "Really. This one says Wildflower Mountain Mining Company, and this one . . ." She grabbed for another, "Look, it says Hiram W. Clayton, and look at the press—Denver, Colorado, 1905."

"That's it, I'm going to radio the sheriff." Davenport headed toward the mine entrance.

"You do that," Gretchen called after him, "I haven't seen my cousin Cody since Aunt Natalie's birthday right after Christmas."

"Davenport! What are you trying to pull here?" It was Doc Stanton talking.

118

He stopped in his tracks, and turned. "Do I know you?"

"You should," Doc continued, "you've been bringing me the *Wall Street Journal* every Monday all summer."

"This is nuts!" Davenport stormed. "Were you part of that gang down at the rodeo that tried to steal my gold shipment?"

"Steal it?" Crystal almost roared. "I was the one who risked my life to stop the stagecoach and rescue your gold."

"So you *are* mixed up in this. But you can't con me out of it. It's my gold!" Davenport shouted.

"Our gold, you mean," one of the gray-suited men interjected.

"Gentlemen," Doc said, "maybe I can offer my services. I'm Howard Stanton, M.I.T., class of '44. For thirty-five years professor of geology, and lately retired old prospector up in these hills. What kind of reports have you received from the assay office?"

"Well, none yet, but . . ." the deep-voiced man admitted.

"Allow me to give you a short lesson in geology," Doc began.

"Wait a minute!" Davenport interrupted. "Any person on the face of the globe can claim to be a geology expert. How in the world do we know if you're legitimate?"

Doc Stanton grinned. "Well now, it seems to me that anybody can come in here to the Pine Mill with some papers and claim to own a mine. How do I know you are who you say you are?"

Davenport continued walking toward the entrance, shouting, "This is getting us nowhere. I'm calling the sheriff no matter whose cousin he is."

"Wait!" one of the businessmen yelled. "Hold on, Davenport. Let's not get in a hurry. We'd like to hear what this man has to say. Besides, if you call in the law, count us gone. This money is ah, well, better left out of public view."

Another man added, "Why do you think we brought cash? We're not about to have the government snooping into our books."

The first man turned to Doc. "Now, if you'll talk some geology to us—"

"Did you run a test on this metal?" Doc Stanton pointed toward a lump of rock sitting on a ledge.

"Of course we did, and it proved to be about sixty percent pure gold. That's top quality," the man said firmly.

"Oh, I don't know," Doc countered. "That makes it about fourteen-carat gold. You can buy that at any jewelry store. In fact, the price of jewelry's been down lately. Is that the Aqua Regia test?"

"Uh, yeah. So what?" said the deep-voiced man.

"That will tell you something about the gold, but it doesn't tell you about the alloy it's mixed with. The hydrochloric and nitric acids don't give you a reading on the alloy," Doc concluded.

"What does this mountain man know?" Davenport protested. "I've consulted with experts."

"Just wait, Davenport," several of the men demurred. "Let's hear the old man out."

Doc Stanton continued. "Gold jewelry is mixed with silver, but the gold in these mines is strictly quartz. Look at the sides of this shaft. Now, if I found fourteen-carat gold mixed with silver, I'd suspect I was looking at someone's melted-down earrings. Did you test the gold up there at the ceiling?"

"No, we didn't. Couldn't reach it," the deep-voiced man explained.

"Of course not, and it's a good thing because that's no more gold than my shoes. Pure gold veins like that's supposed to be exist in the minds of dreamers and schemers. Where's the quartz? It takes this old earth producing extreme temperatures to come up with gold. That's why it's mixed with other metals. But not up there; look at it hanging as pretty as a picture."

Crystal decided it was her turn. "Besides, this whole rock pile's a phony. From the backside where I was, it's just chicken wire and cement." Crystal grabbed a hammer she saw in the corner and climbed the rocks. She got up as high as she could and banged away. A chunk of the cement soon gave way and exposed the wire framework underneath.

A voice she recognized as Sidney's said, "Okay, Davenport, I've heard enough. We're taking our money back. Where'd he go?"

Davenport had disappeared. "He's got the duffel

bag of money!" one of them yelled. "We've got to catch him before he reaches that helicopter!"

The five men in suits, Gretchen, Doc, and Crystal rushed along the horizontal shaft to the entrance. The slick leather shoes of the businessmen slipped on the rough granite floor. Shouts, yells, and curses echoed through the tunnel. Crystal and Doc were the first to reach the large sheet metal building in front of the entrance.

A familiar, terrifying sound greeted them. "The dogs!" Crystal cried. "He's locked them in this building!"

The two guard dogs snapped at them until Gretchen caught up. "Come here, you big mutt," she ordered the biggest of the two as she stepped forward.

"Gretchen," Crystal called in fright.

"I know dogs almost like I know horses," Gretchen assured her. "This one's a cream puff. Come on over here," she called out, "and I'll scratch your head." She ruffled the dog's ears, and he just whimpered.

Crystal cautiously stepped forward. "What about this one?"

"He's a team dog. No partner, no bite. But he might growl at you." Gretchen now had the big one down on its side, scratching its stomach.

Doc and Crystal ventured past the snarling, but stationary dog. As the five men behind them did the same, Gretchen released the big dog. "Go back," she told him.

Immediately he resumed his position with the other dog. They both barked furiously at the men.

"Hey, how about us?" Sidney yelled.

"We'll be back," Gretchen called back as she joined Doc and Crystal outisde.

"We'll never stop a helicopter," Crystal wailed as they ran to the landing sight. Then she stopped. A whole group of men stood around the helicopter. There was Bucky and a deputy sheriff and Hank and—"Dad! Shawn!" she hollered.

When Crystal reached them, her dad said quickly, "We just this minute got here. What's happened to you? Hank was just about to take us into the mine shaft after you." He looked her up and down. "Are you all right?"

"I'm fine, Dad. Did you guys see a man running out here carrying a duffel bag? It's full of money that doesn't belong to him."

"Whose money is it?" the deputy interrogated.

"Some men out of Spokane," Doc explained. "It sounds to me like it's laundered money. They didn't want the police in on it. Cash, you know."

"Cash?" The deputy repeated. "How much?'

As Crystal's eyes searched the surrounding area, she replied, "I think it's $250,000."

The deputy took charge. "Spread out and scour these grounds. Is he armed?" he asked.

"I don't think so," Crystal answered. "But I don't know for sure.

"Bucky, you stay and watch the helicopter," the deputy continued.

Crystal gave her dad a big hug. "I'm really glad to see you," she said as they joined the others in the search.

They circled the buildings once, and found nothing. "Is there another way out of here?" the deputy asked Hank.

"Well, I don't think so," he said.

"I know!" Crystal shouted. "Down the canyon. The old mine road we came up. Davenport must have hiked that trail all summer, so of course he knows about it. But he might not know that we know."

The whole party began to run up the granite slope to the trees at the canyon's edge. Crystal mounted Caleb. Shawn jumped up behind her. They quickly passed the others and were the first to reach the edge. They could see one of Gretchen's horses down the cliff. The other was missing.

"Down there, look!" Crystal hollered. "There he is with Gretchen's horse!"

Shawn slipped off Caleb. "I'll ride the other one. You wait for the others and follow on foot," he suggested.

"Wait, Shawn, I want to go." She jumped off Caleb and climbed down the cliff. But Shawn hadn't heard her.

Meanwhile the big gray Appaloosa appeared at the edge of the trees where overgrowth blocked the old road. He leaped a large rock, then ducked under a sloping tree trunk, sidestepped a couple logs, and ran to Crystal's side. "Caleb!" she squealed.

124

"So that's how you did it! Good boy, good boy!" she mounted and kissed his neck. He glanced back, but looked unimpressed. Crystal spurred him down the steep trail.

Mr. Blake and the others reached the cliff just as she turned the first corner. She pretended not to hear their shouts.

There was no fast way of retreat. The trail took time by foot or horseback. But Caleb moved well. Crystal had a chance or two to glance across the box canyon as she descended. The sun was setting on the western peaks, giving a rose pink glow to the scene. She spotted Shawn up ahead. His horse balked at crossing Crystal's makeshift rock crossing. He had dismounted. "Can't get him to cross," Shawn complained when he heard her coming. "Will Caleb?"

Crystal didn't bother to reply. She rode Caleb to the other side, then looked back at Shawn in triumph. "Still can't get this animal to move," he confessed.

Shawn ran across alone. "I'll leave him there for Gretchen." He hopped behind Crystal once more.

The floor of the canyon was flooded with shadows as they reached the flatland. They'd seen no rider. "Let's cut by the house and pick up another horse," Shawn suggested. "I'd guess he'd go up the trail to Elk City and look for a way out of town."

Crystal didn't hurry Caleb. She knew he must be as tired as she was. Shawn ran for the barn while Crystal headed for Gretchen's tack room. She couldn't believe one woman owned so many saddles. She grabbed one that looked like hers and struggle to carry it back to Shawn. Soon they headed out of Gretchen's lane.

They arrived at the narrow gap of the box canyon with still no sight of Davenport. At the beach area next to the river Shawn proposed that they split up. "We can't really track a horse in this soft sand," he explained.

She followed the river's edge, and he cut across the sand for the trail to Elk City. His parting words were, "Whoever sees him hollers for the other."

Crystal still wouldn't run Caleb. A cold wind whistled down the canyon to where they idled along, refreshing them both. She let Caleb stop for a drink. That's when she caught sight of Davenport riding hard in the distance across the sand toward the river. "Shawn must have cut him off," she said to Caleb as his head jerked up.

Davenport's horse, which had been ridden hard, hit the edge of the water, then halted. As Crystal approached, she heard Davenport shout and kick to no avail. "Looks like too much of a river for any horse, to me," said Crystal to herself. "A current like that—but Davenport's only got to drift downstream to get away!" she exclaimed.

She saw Shawn approach, but she didn't wait. She kicked Caleb and for the first time in two days, she saw him perk up. He plunged right into the water towards the fleeing Davenport, who had dismounted.

126

The icy water reached Crystal's knees as Davenport tried to keep ahead of Caleb. The big gray intimidated the man to head back towards shore. If Davenport aimed for deeper water, Caleb cut him off. Crystal rode and watched. Then it dawned on her. Caleb was herding Davenport like a stray cow. "Big, old Caleb," she mused. "Give him a prodigal to round up, and he's like a kid with a new toy."

Shawn held the reins of Davenport's borrowed horse on the shore as Caleb kept pushing the man back upstream. By now Davenport was drained of strength. At one point, Caleb got so close he nosed Davenport, which caused the swindler to slide downstream a few feet and lose his grip on the duffel bag. They watched it float through the white water rapids of the Salmon River.

Davenport screamed, "That's my money!"

He tried to dive after it, but Caleb prevented him. With the money now gone, Davenport changed tactics. He splashed towards the beach.

Shawn rushed to remount. Caleb was soon out of the water and pulling his weight across the loose sand.

Heading towards Gretchen's ranch, Davenport quickly was surrounded by Mr. Blake, Doc, and Gretchen coming down the gap on horseback. Davenport raced toward the mountains instead. Caleb veered to the left forcing him back to the sand. Shawn covered him on the right. Finally Davenport dropped right in front of Crystal and Caleb.

Crystal stayed on her horse, waiting for the others to come. Davenport floundered, then flopped back down. Suddenly Shawn screamed, "Crystal! Look out!"

Caleb reared on his hind legs, and Crystal threw her hands around his neck to hold on. It was then she saw the gun Davenport held.

She went into hysterics. "No! Not Caleb! Don't shoot Caleb!"

10

BACK TO THE REAL WORLD

PANIC SEIZED CRYSTAL. ALL THE PRESSURES AND stress of the day came to a head. She clenched Caleb's neck tighter than she'd gripped anything in her life.

She was still crying and clutching Caleb when her dad pried her from the horse and carried her in his arms. His strong embrace rocked her back and forth. "Daddy," she gasped several times. "He was going to shoot Caleb! And I'm so tired!"

"I know, princess. I know, it's okay now, just rest," he comforted.

Crystal wasn't sure how long her dad cradled her like that. When she relaxed enough to look up she saw Shawn, Doc, and Gretchen circled around the sprawled-out Davenport whose feet and hands were tied. Doc walked over to them and handed Crystal a neatly folded white handkerchief. "I promise it's unused. Maybe it will help a little."

Crystal tried her best to clean her face, and then she and her dad walked over to the others. "Sorry for that scene," she said quietly, her eyes down. "When I saw that gun, well, I'd had enough adventures. I didn't want to show off my horse riding

129

anymore. I just wanted to take Caleb away from there. I guess I've gotten pretty attached to him."

"What surprised me," Doc said, "was you didn't seem worried any about yourself. He could have shot you just as well."

"Doc," Gretchen answered, "it's horse sense. You either got it, or you don't. I knew just how she felt. After a while there's a bond that can't be described. That big old gray lunk would break his back trying to take care of this young lady, and a girl with horse sense, well, she'd do the same for him. No one on this earth ever won a ropin' or ridin' event without it."

"What happened to the gun?" Crystal asked.

"Shawn has it," her father reported.

"No, I mean, why didn't he shoot it?" Crystal pressed.

Shawn looked over the short-nosed revolver. "But he did! It just clicked. Apparently he had this thing in a small holster strapped to his leg. He couldn't get to it out in the river."

"It didn't fire because it was too wet?" Crystal questioned.

"Nope, he was just too out of it to remember that the safety was on. And then your dad flew off his horse and clobbered the guy," Shawn said with admiration.

Crystal couldn't say any more for a few minutes.

Gretchen broke the silence. "What do you say we take our capture over to my place and radio the sheriff? He'll tell us what to do next."

They all scurried into action. Mr. Blake and Doc lifted the dazed Davenport across Shawn's horse. His feet hung on one side of the saddle, and his head on the other. Once more, a very weary Crystal climbed on Caleb, with Shawn behind her. She was too exhausted even to care how messy she looked.

The little troop took an easy pace across the sandy beach and into the narrow canyon trail. This was Gretchen's world, and she took charge.

In front of the cabin they left Davenport sprawled across the saddle. They followed Gretchen to the back room and huddled around the radio as she started the generator. She explained to Crystal and Shawn that the deputy and Bucky had taken the five businessmen back to Elk City.

Crystal turned in her chair. "Shouldn't someone be with Davenport? He'll try to get away."

Gretchen twisted radio knobs as she said, "Honey, I've been hog-tying cattle for fifty-two of my fifty-five years, and not one—not one ever got away. He's as safe as money in the bank." She smiled. "Safer. Bucky, this is Gretchen. Do you read me? Bucky?" she barked into the mike.

"Bucky here," came the swift reply. "The sheriff's with me. We've got every trail out of the canyon blocked, plus an a.p.b. on Davenport in five western states. Listen, Gretchen, be careful. The sheriff already ran a check on him. He's wanted down in Houston on a silver swindle, and he's usually armed."

"Hold on," Gretchen cracked back across the airwaves. "Tell Cody to send the troops home. We've got Davenport out of commission here at the ranch. Crystal and the big Appy of hers ran him down. Just tell me what you want me to do."

There was a pause, then a new voice came on. "Gretchen, this is Cody, do you read me?"

"Hi, Sheriff, how's Aunt Natalie?" Gretchen switched the radio back to receive.

"Fine, fine. Listen, you remember when I deputized you a couple years back when we had trouble with those guys pirating salmon? As far as the books go, you're still a deputy. So I'm leaving this guy in your custody until the break of day. It's too dark to get down there tonight, and we wouldn't want you making the trail either. Tie him to a tree or something. We'll bring a chopper in first thing. Can you handle that?"

"A piece of cake," Gretchen thundered. "And one more thing, Davenport carried some money in a satchel." She turned to Crystal. "What color was it?"

"It was a dark green duffel bag," she told Gretchen.

"Cody, it was dark green, last seen floating down the river towards Squawman's Crossing. You might send some men downstream to look for it."

"Okay," Cody came back on, "how much money arc we talking?"

"Check with your so-called respectable business friends from Spokane. Davenport claimed there

132

was a quarter of a million—cash."

A clamor of noise came over the radio. Then Cody responded, "If this gets out, it'll start another Idaho stampede. Keep it quiet, and I'll be on your beach by sunup."

"Breaker, breaker . . . this is Big Jim from Silver City . . . calling for Crystal LuAnne Blake."

Gretchen raised her eyebrows. "Have you been using the radio?"

"Not successfully," Crystal sighed, and took the mike. "Big Jim, this is Crystal."

"Crystal, baby. This is Big Jim down in New Mexico. Remember our nice little chat earlier today? Well, did I hear mention of big piles of dough floating in some river your way?"

"Uh, I'm, I'm not sure what you thought you heard," Crystal hemmed and hawed.

"Well, could you just tell me one thing? Suppose a guy drove up to Idaho from the south, just exactly which highway would come closest to that river?"

"I have no idea in the world. I'm from southern California myself. Bye, bye, Big Jim."

"Hold it—hold it!"

Gretchen flipped the off switch as they all had a good laugh. Then Gretchen organized her impromptu crew as they walked to the front porch. "Doc, you go out to that shed behind the barn. There's two milk cows back there that's dying to see someone. The bucket's there in the kitchen. Shawn, you take care of the horses. Make sure that

133

Caleb gets a good rubdown. Mr. Blake, if you will, take this broom and sweep out the bunkhouse." She pointed to a long, narrow building to the right of the cabin. "It's not been used since a fire-fighting crew was down here several years back. You men will have to bunk it out tonight. I've only got room for us ladies in the house."

"What about him?" Shawn looked at Davenport.

"Take him out to the barn. I've got a set of iron horse hobbles there. Fasten them on him, and chain him to the anvil. Give him a little straw for sleeping. I'll feed him later if we have any leftovers. It's been awhile since I've cooked for a gang."

"What about me?" Crystal said. "What do you want me to do?"

"Fire up that stove and get the hot water boiling. You're going to take a bath! There's no way I'm going to let something as grubby as you sit at my supper table."

Crystal was out of the tub and drying her clean hair when Gretchen knocked. "You decent?"

Crystal looked in the mirror. "Well, I'm clean, anyway."

Gretchen carried in a yellow dress on a hanger. She hooked it on the back of the door. "Thought you might like wearing a dress for a change. I've had this since '49, but these western dresses never go out of style. They still make them just the same. Can you believe I used to fit into that?" Gretchen chuckled. "I've kept it in the closet just waiting for the day I'd lose thirty pounds."

134

"It looks great. Thanks, Gretchen."

"Hurry along, if you can. The men are through with their chores, and making lots of noise about being hungry."

Crystal wasn't sure how attractive the dress was on her, but it certainly made her feel prettier. The gathered skirt flowed out full when she twirled around. She pushed the puffy short sleeves up on her arms and twirled again. She quickly looked in the mirror and walked out to the kitchen.

Doc whistled.

Shawn teased. "She has blonde hair. I didn't know her hair was blonde." Her dad joined in the teasing.

"All right, you jerks," she giggled, "don't you know a lady when you see one?"

"You tell them, Crystal," Gretchen said as she carried another bowl to the table. "Now, everyone, find a place. The bad news is, I didn't have time to bake us a huckleberry pie. We'll just have to eat them with a little fresh cream. But the good news is there are big steaks, garden fresh carrots, beans, and corn, plus mashed potatoes and red-eye gra-vy—enough to feed a roundup.

"Mr. Blake," Gretchen started as she sat down, "I wonder if I could call upon you to say grace. I can hear myself pray any old time."

They all bowed their heads.

"Lord," he began, "it's been a busy day. We probably didn't spend a lot of time remembering you. But, Lord, we sure are grateful you remem-

135

bered us. Thank you, Lord, for being with Crystal and Caleb and the others as they traveled up and down the canyon. Thanks for dogs that didn't bite, guns that didn't fire, and horses that didn't panic. Thanks for your love that surrounds us and holds us tight in the toughest times. Thanks for the experiences of this day that brought all of us together. And thank you for Gretchen's generosity. Give us your strength and peace. In Jesus' name. Amen and amen."

The meal started out subdued. They ate quietly, caught in their own thoughts. Halfway through her steak, Crystal broke the silence. "Hey, if Davenport had a million dollars' worth of gold on the stage, why did he need financial backers? Or even a scam?"

Shawn swallowed and answered, "I was talking out in the barn with Davenport about that. He admitted the gold buttons were phonies. Just some cement with thin gold leaf. Seems he started out to make two million. He planned to have the shipment stolen, then claim the insurance to cover its loss. He actually leaked out the information about the shipment. He's been bragging about it since he came to."

"That way, it couldn't be assayed," Gretchen added.

Shawn continued. "Yes, and at the same time he set up the sting for the businessmen. He found out which ones might have hidden funds. That way he'd avoid the authorities. Old Hank got suckered

136

in to add credibility. He hoped for five hundred thousand to a million out of the men. But, when the buttons were not stolen, he had to act fast and get their money before they were discovered to be phonies. That's why he settled for the $250,000. He was getting desperate."

"Seems to me," Doc said, "that some folks work harder at not working than the rest of us do at working."

"Shawn!" Crystal suddenly sat up straight. "What are you doing here, anyway?"

"My dad brought Grandpa home to Winchester, so I came up with my horse. There's a rodeo tomorrow night in Nez Perce, and I thought I'd do some roping."

Crystal's dad took seconds on green beans as he continued the conversation. "I was in Winchester right after noon and brought Shawn up with me. We were at Bucky's when Gretchen radioed."

"Yes, and listen to this, Crystal," Shawn added. "My dad went over to Highland High School, our old foes, and talked to them about a job. They have an opening, and he's actually considering moving us up to Winchester. He wants to be closer to Grandpa. Can you beat that? After all my life in Riggins, I might be moving. I'm not sure I like that," he concluded.

Crystal smiled to herself, thinking, "And no more Terri Biggers." She turned to her dad, "Yesterday morning you said you had a secret to tell me. What was that all about?"

"Well, young lady, I do," Mr. Blake responded. "However, I'd rather sit out on the porch with a big bowl of huckleberries and cream to tell you about it. What do you say? You about finished?"

"Yes, just about," she replied. "Gretchen, this might be the best meal in the whole wide world."

The others mumbled agreement.

Gretchen nodded, too. "That's what I think about every meal out here."

Shawn carried some food out to Davenport, and Doc and Gretchen cleared the table. Crystal and her dad took their berries out into the still Idaho evening. They could hear the roar of the river rushing far down below.

"Dad, is Mom pregnant again?" Crystal guessed.

"What?" he gasped. "What made you think that?"

"The last time you sat me down to tell me a secret was before Allyson was born. Remember?"

"No, that's not it. Listen, Crystal, your mom and I have had a dream for several years. And now, with that advance coming in, it looks like it's time to go for it. We'd like to move out of southern California and build a place in the mountains somewhere. A place that fits our writing style. Some peaceful, quiet place where the air's pure and the folks are friendly. I know this comes on you all of a sudden, and that's why I wanted to talk to you in private. There's no way we'll consider it if you and Karla don't want to move."

"Move? Really? You want to move?" The

138

thought opened up new avenues Crystal had never considered before.

"Well, that's the secret. What do you think so far?"

"What does Karla think? Did you talk to Karla yet? It's her senior year and everything."

"She's ready to move this weekend," her dad assured her. "I think she's fed up with Citrus Valley High."

"But where to? Do you have a spot in mind?" Crystal's mind raced ahead of her words. "Like up here? Are you thinking of Idaho?"

"Would you believe Winchester, Idaho?" He grinned.

"Winchester? You mean where Shawn's going? Would we live close to Shawn?" She began to plan the next several years in a matter of seconds.

"Not exactly next door. But you remember when we visited there on Sunday? It's not very big—only 350 people or so."

"Did you find a house already?" she asked.

"Oh, no, not until everyone approves. Besides, I want us to build a house just like we want."

"Is it all up to me, then?"

"Pretty much so. Your mother and Karla are ready. And you know Allyson will be happy anywhere we are."

"As long as she has her blanket," Crystal smiled, as she started to miss her two-year-old sister.

"You don't have to decide tonight. Just think it through," he said. "I found some property on the edge of town. I sent to Spokane to get some financial things arranged, in case we decide to do it. This property's on the high side of town, covered with pine trees, overlooking the lake. There's no road in there yet, but the town will put one in if we build. Hey, and get this—on the backside of the property is a nice clearing about the size of a good barn and pasture."

"For Caleb!" Crystal rejoined. "Does Highland High have a rodeo team?"

"Sure do, but they didn't do so well this year. Things look much better for next year, however. There're rumors a hotshot roper from Riggins and a beach bunny from sunny California with one terrific Appaloosa may be moving in."

"Okay, you convinced me. I want to move. But what will I tell Megan?"

Mr. Blake stood and stretched. "Tell her to come spend the summers with us."

"Really?"

"Sure, now let's get to bed. We'll talk some more about it in the morning."

The roar of a helicopter overhead brought Crystal to consciousness. She wrenched herself out of the feather bed, pulled on some jeans and her last clean shirt, and walked to the porch barefoot.

Gretchen was there looking up at the helicopter. "Where is everyone?" Crystal asked.

"The men took Davenport to the beach to meet the sheriff. Come on in, you need some breakfast. The others have eaten."

140

"Why didn't you wake me?" she questioned.

"I tried to wake you two times, and your dad tried several more. We thought maybe you planned to skip today." Gretchen held the door open.

The two sat down at the big table. Gretchen sipped hot coffee as Crystal ate. "Gretchen," Crystal said between bites of biscuits and gravy, "we were so busy yesterday, I forgot to ask. How long have you known Doc Stanton?" Crystal brushed the hair behind her ears. "I mean, he seems like a nice guy to me."

"Well, I've known Doc since . . . well, I think it was around noon yesterday."

"You mean, the two of you never met before?" Crystal said with wide eyes.

"Nope, we just ran across each other on the trail and found we had a mutual friend." She grinned.

"Oh, who?" Crystal thought she knew the answer.

"Her name's Crystal Blake. Ever heard of her?"

Crystal laughed, "The famous barrel racer."

"One and the same." Gretchen paused slightly. "And you know, we seem to hit it off real well."

Crystal raised her eyebrows. "Is he leaning anywhere towards perfect?"

"Honey, he's a lot closer to perfect than I am. If this one gets away, it won't be because I didn't give it a good chase." They both laughed.

The men soon returned from the beach. Gretchen and Crystal joined them outside at the horse rail. "So you got him off?" Gretchen inquired.

"No problems except the reporters," Mr. Blake answered.

"Reporters?" Crystal said in amazement. "You mean I missed getting my picture taken and all? Did you tell them about Caleb? They should at least have taken a photo of him."

"Hey," Shawn interrupted, "they weren't interested in you, in me, or Caleb. All they asked was, 'Where did you last see the duffel bag full of money?'"

"They must have taken a million pictures just of the river," Doc responded.

Mr. Blake got off his horse. "Crystal, get your gear and your horse. It's time to return to the real world. We've got to settle up with Bucky, then get Shawn over to his grandfather's."

"We're heading back to California already?"

"First, we have to do some shopping. I need some after shave, aspirin, carob almonds, and three lots and a pasture in Winchester, and of course, your boots." Mr. Blake looked at her for affirmation. "What do you say, kiddo? Do you still want to move?"

Crystal nodded.

"Okay, that's what we'll do. As a soon-to-be-famous writer always says, 'I must do those things in life I would regret not doing.'" Crystal repeated the phrase with him.

"What did you say about buying boots?" Crystal asked.

"I figured you didn't want to enter the junior

barrel racing over at Nez Perce tonight without wearing boots," her dad responded.

"Junior rodeo? Hey, no way. I told Gretchen yesterday I couldn't do that," Crystal protested. "I mean, Caleb's a good horse. But I don't even know what I'm doing. And besides, I'm not very fast. Some ten-year-old will beat me. There's no way you're going to get Crystal LuAnne Blake to compete in front of a crowd of people."

Mr. Blake looked at Shawn and winked.